City of Kingz

Chris Green

**Lock Down Publications and Ca$h
Presents**
City of Kingz
A Novel by *Chris Green*

Chris Green

Lock Down Publications
P.O. Box 944
Stockbridge, Ga 30281

Visit our website @
www.lockdownpublications.com

Copyright 2020 by Chris Green
City of Kingz

Lock Down Publications
Like our page on Facebook: Lock Down
Publications @
www.facebook.com/lockdownpublications.ldp
Cover design and layout by: **Dynasty Cover Me**
Book interior design by: **Shawn Walker**
Edited by: **Shamika Smith**

Stay Connected with Us!

Text **LOCKDOWN** to 22828 to stay up-to-date with new releases, sneak peaks, contests and more...

Thank you.

Submission Guideline.

Submit the first three chapters of your completed manuscript to ldpsubmissions@gmail.com, subject line: Your book's title. The manuscript must be in a .doc file and sent as an attachment. Document should be in Times New Roman, double spaced and in size 12 font. Also, provide your synopsis and full contact information. If sending multiple submissions, they must each be in a separate email.

Have a story but no way to send it electronically? You can still submit to LDP/Ca$h Presents. Send in the first three chapters, written or typed, of your completed manuscript to:

LDP: Submissions Dept
P.O. Box 944
Stockbridge, Ga 30281

DO NOT send original manuscript. Must be a duplicate.

Provide your synopsis and a cover letter containing your full contact information.

Thanks for considering LDP and Ca$h Presents.

Dedication

This book is dedicated to myself. I've learned a valuable lesson in the midst of writing this novel. I've learned that you can try to help all the people you possibly can when you're in position to. But it doesn't breed true loyalty. They will use you to their advantage in order to come up or achieve whatever they can. To shorten things up and make it clear, I'm striving and pushing through this bid alone. The steps I'm making to change have been taken on my own. I've been used, left, and and lied to for over nine years of incarceration. I accept it, and I forgive those who perpetrated those transgressions against me. But I refuse to keep allowing the same fumbles to hinder my heart, and my emotions.

From now on, I'm focusing on me and my family. I'm focused on success. This book is one of my best, storyline-wise. I'm excited to say that it has given me an entire new frame of mind. If you read CITY OF KINGZ, please be kind enough to leave a review on Amazon or whatever site you purchased it from.

Love goes out to my baby Cerenity. My mama Dolsellia. My sister Shanika. My most loved, and bestfriend Lana. My brother Deangelo. My uncle and aunts. My grandma's, and all the close associates of the Green family. I love you all. Thank you. #WeRBooks!

Chris Green

Chapter 1

The Reign of Sacramento
Sacramento, California 11:47 P. M.

Silence filled the truck as Keyno pushed the black GMC Terrain to their destination. Glancing in the rearview mirror, he observed Jabari's stiff posture. Knowing that it was his first time going on the jack move, he wanted to be sure the young kid didn't crash out if things happened to go left field."

"You look nervous. You a'ight, lil bro?"

"I'm good, Keyno. You ain't gotta keep second guessing me, man."

Smiling at Jabari's arrogance. He placed his attention back on the road.

"Well, I hope you ain't scared nigga. I ain't got time to be taking up nobody slack," Blow added while placing the clip into his AR-15.

"I ain't scared of shit."

Turning around in the passenger seat to face Jabari, Blow stared in his eyes to see if he would break. "You say that shit now. I bet you ain't got enough heart to pop a nigga's shit loose if anybody get messy in this bitch. It's easy to rob a nigga that'll give up the check without a fight. Try taking from a nigga who's willing to die."

Jabari disregarded his hating ass words and continued to focus on the mission at hand. He needed this money. Before he backed out like a bitch, he was willing to die for the sake of his little brother eating and having the necessities to survive.

Keyno pulled inside of the small driveway of the home about fifteen minutes later. Turning around in the front seat to look at Jabari, he pulled a chain from around his neck. On the end was a dog tag that had 'Trust' engraved in the middle. Placing it around Jabari's neck for him, he smiled. "Listen, no matter what you do, don't fold. Be sure to follow me. If you follow me, you'll always win. Okay?" Keyno made sure he understood.

Jabari nodded his head in a fast motion. "I'm ready. Trust me."

Keyno flashed a wry smile as he stepped out of the car with Blow and Jabari directly behind him. There wasn't a need for any masks because you only did what you meant in the state of California. Sacramento to be specific. Everyone was about their issue, and if you wasn't, then you were bound to be consumed by the hands of your own environment.

After easing up the small parking lot, Keyno placed a slug in the chamber of his AK-47. Blow was dressed in all black with his hair tied straight to the back in a rubber band. The look on his face said that he was about to cause a fucking scene, and Jabari stood in the back with a black hoodie tied over his head. Not sure if he could handle the large assault rifle, he settled for a Glock 18 handgun. Keyno placed his ear to the door and could hear the music bumping. You could tell these were some older motherfuckas because Maxwell's "Pretty Wings" was bumping like it was the new YG album inside that bitch.

Blow watched Keyno smile and knock on the door with four sharp knocks. That's when he slid his skullcap down low and aimed his AR-15 just in case he had to smoke one of these bitch ass niggas.

The sound of a man's voice boomed on the other side. "Password?"

Keyno steadied his gun and answered. "Let's make a fortune."

The locks shifting on the other side caused the boys to tense up. When the door opened slightly, Keyno raised his foot, and kicked, causing it to cave in the older man's face forcefully.

Rushing inside first, he wasted no time killing the first guard who raised his gun.

Pak! Pak! Pak!

"Get the fuck down if you don't wanna motherfucking die!"

The look on Jabari's face instantly changed when he witnessed the man's brains leaking from his skull. He couldn't fake it as if that shit didn't rattle his nerves. Still, he held his gun high and stood right beside Keyno without saying a word.

The small gambling home was easy to settle when Blow laid the entire poker card table down. One by one, six men were placed on the floor with a zip tie to bound them still. Stacks of hundreds sat in bundles on the spade table, and the two women who held the kitty pot was holding their hands high where Keyno could see them. His 6'3" 240-pound frame was straight muscle, and he wouldn't hesitate to use it if necessary.

"This the wrong house, Lil Jack. We don't take robberies lightly, son," Mr. Jubbie said as Blow zip tied his wrist, and feet.

"Oh yeah? Well guess what, Mr. Jubbie? You finally getting yo bitch ass robbed today. We told you that this shit wasn't impossible, old man." Blow chuckled before dismissing the elder's threat.

Mr. Jubbie was a known killer back in the day who ate off the block for years. After heading to Pelican Bay for a fifteen-year bid, he returned home at the age of forty-six. He began moving small weight and establishing gambling houses around the city. The old man had so much money that the jackers in the hood felt as if he was now a free pick. Everyone who tested his gangsta ended up dead or found diced up in the nearest trash can. He was ruthless, but when it came down to Keyno and Blow, they considered it the lick of the year. The two of them together terrorized Sacramento on all sides. Robbing, Murdering, whatever it took to get that mighty dollar.

Keyno handed Jabari a giant trash bag. "Go grab all the cash, and everything valuable you see. Check their pockets and take it all," he whispered.

Nodding with nervousness flowing through his bones, he moved pass Blow and headed straight for the poker table. The rolls of money was like ice cream to a small child on a summer day. Jabari had never seen so much cash in his life. Quickly picking up the paper, he stuffed it into the bag until the table was completely empty. A few pieces of jewelry laid around, and he was even sure to stuff that into the bag as well. Once he was done, he moved over to the spade table.

Keyno pointed the AK-47 at the two hood bitches. "Y'all hoes keep ya hands up and raise ya head up to the ceiling. If anyone of y'all move, I'ma blow ya esophagus to Puerto Rico."

The women obliged, and damn sure wasn't trying to get hit with none of the exclusive ass artillery they was toting. When Jabari got to the spade table, his eyes couldn't even total the amount of paper, he was scanning at the time. All he knew for sure was the payday was damn sure a nice one. Stuffing every coin inside of the bag, he made his way back over to the men on the floor and began to run their pockets.

"Keyno, I've got respect for you, young blood. This isn't true games you wanna play with me, son. My name is Mr. Jubbie, and I'm an old playa in this hood. You can't get away with shit like this. Now on the strength of you being a young known hoodlum, I'll allow this to slide. If you put the money back and leave, I'll give you something to put on your pockets to call it even. Taking my shit though," Mr. Jubbie shook his head with his lips curled like a snake. "That shit means a nigga gotta die, son."

"Sit that nigga up, Blow," Keyno ordered.

Jabari finished clearing the pockets and stood back by the door while Keyno moved over to the elderly ma and bent down. Mr. Jubbie glared into his eyes, as if he was prepared to die.

"Look old man. When you hear Keyno's name that means I'm taking. That's the reason I move around with no hiding. Maybe you need to do more research on me. I've been killing niggas of yo status since I was sixteen. I'm thirty-one now, so I know you get the point. This money is mines, and if you want smoke about it, you know where to find me." Keyno smiled arrogantly.

Blow, and Keyno was so focused on the men in front of them, the they never saw the woman who reached for the double barrel pump under the spade's table. Jabari's eyes turned to see her just as she cocked a shell into the chamber. His mind stiffened, and he could see that see was aiming straight for the back of Keyno's head. Before she could lift that bitch, Jabari raised his Glock 18 and released over seven shots into her chest.

Boc! Boc! Boc! Boc! Boc! Boc! Boc!

Her body was slightly smoking from the slugs and she caved over to the floor, falling face first. Keyno jumped to his feet and spotted exactly what was going on. Raising his gun at the other woman's face, he released shot into her throat.

Pak!

"Punk ass bitches just tried to kill me!" His eyes looked over to Jabari who still aimed the pistol with a paranoid face. His hands were trembling and Keyno could tell that he was shook from what just happened.

"Jabari, it's okay lil one. Relax."

All he could do was nod, but he damn sure didn't lower his gun.

Keyno turned around and looked at Blow whose chest was heaving with anger. "Have fun nigga. What you waiting for?"

Hearing Keyno's approval, Blow aimed his choppa at all the men who were lined up and riddled their bodies with bullets.

Boc! Boc! Boc! Boc! Boc! Boc! Boc!

Keyno stepped closer to Mr. Jubbie who was now panting in fear. "Don't do this young blood. I said we can work this out," he pleaded like he was short of breath.

"You should have thought about that before yo smoker just tried to take me out," Keyno spat as he raised the gun and placed three bullets directly through his heart.

Pak! Pak! Pak!

Mr. Jubbie's hand reached for his chest, but unfortunately that shit was long gone. Folding over on the floor. Keyno headed for the door with the quickness. "Two minutes are up. We're out this bitch," he ordered before all three of them took flight out of the home.

The sound of Keyno's truck could be heard smashing out of the driveway, leaving the massacre behind for forensics to investigate. The silence in Mr. Jubbie's spot was quieter than a mouse until one of the men slightly coughed and began to breath harshly.

* * *

Making it back to the Jabari's side of town, Keyno pulled the car on the side of his father's home. Killing the ignition, he stepped out of the driver seat, as Jabari climbed out of the back.

"Hey, are you okay?" Keyno playfully hit him in the chest. He could tell that Jabari catching his first body was fucking with his mental. Truth be told, he was happier than anything because if he wouldn't of fired that strap, he could've been left behind with all the other motherfuckers who was slumped tonight.

"I'm good, Keyno. That shit was just kind of crazy. Ya know?" His head was held low as if he did something wrong.

Keyno pulled the large roll of money from his back pocket and mashed it against his chest. "Don't regret what happened tonight, lil one. You did good. If you wouldn't have pulled that fucking trigger, I would've probably died. That's twenty-thousand dollars. Something that a lot of seventeen-year-olds never seen in their whole life. Save some and have fun. You earned it."

Jabari smiled at all the crispy hundreds in his possession. The first night was a bad experience, but through it all, he left with the mission complete. "Damn Keyno. Thanks, big bro. Why you giving me so much? I only bagged up the money."

Keyno smirked. "Trust me, lil one. Ya did more than you know. Just remember from now on to follow me, and you'll always win. We got more in place to make sure you eat. Bigger plates to clean. Now, go ahead and get in the house before your dad wakes up, and try to kill all of us."

"Word. Thanks, Keyno." Jabari walked off towards the back of his home. Before he got a good distance away, he remembered the dog tag chain that was dangling around his neck. Quickly turning around, he whispered, "Keyno, You forgot the chain." Jabari held it up.

Smiling, Keyno winked before jumping back inside the truck. You could hear the Nipsey Hussle's single, "Status Symbol" turn up as he bent the corner.

Jabari couldn't help but smirk. Keyno was that big brother that a nigga could never have, especially with the way he ensured that a young one stayed with something to survive.

Sliding on the edge of his dad's home, Jabari was trying to be sure not to signal the spotlight outside of his bedroom window. Once he was able to succeed and slide pass, he tapped lightly on his little brother's, Brandon, window. His young baby face appeared in the blinds as if he was waiting for him to return. Wasting no time, he released the locks, sliding it up for his older brother to crawl inside.

Once Jabari was safe beyond the walls of his father's home, he locked the window and smiled at his little brother. "What you still doing up?"

"Waiting on you to get back home. I saw you when you left out. Why you didn't let me come, man?" Brandon whispered in the dark.

"Shhhh! You know your little deep voice travels in these thin ass walls. Dad will hear you." Jabari slowly turned on their light, pulling the large bundle of money out of his pocket. He flashed it with a big smile. "This is why I didn't let you come. I had to get you all this!"

Brandon's little young face glowed as if it were Christmas. To be thirteen, he never had over hundred dollars at one time, and that was when their father hit the lottery when decided to let them have a small little amount of fun. It was hard growing up with a poor lifestyle, especially when their dad was a maintenance man who recently came from doing a fifteen-year bid in prison. For the past year, they struggled to have clothes, shoes, and sometimes even food. Their father, Ronald, was a strong individual back in the day who was about his paper. However, after the authorities got ahold of him when they were just children, their lives changed forever.

"Where did you get this Jabari? This is like five thousand dollars," he guessed, adding the money up wrong.

Jabari couldn't help but laugh. His little brother didn't have shit. Even the little pajamas he slept in was too small and dirty as fuck. He needed a new wardrobe and all. The feeling of seeing him go to school every day with worn out hand me downs was about to be over. "It's not five, it's twenty, and it's both of ours. Tomorrow, I'm going to buy you some clothes and shoes. But this is our little secret. If dad asks you anything, just let me handle it." He peeled off five hundred dollars and placed them in his little champ hands. Just that alone made him hug Jabari as if was the end of the world.

"Thanks, Bari. You're the best, bro. Word."

"It's okay, Brandon. That's what I'm here for. I can't give you all this money at once cause I know you'll spend it. Put your money up and get back to bed. School in the a. m."

"Oh yeah!" he beamed with joy. Walking over to the closet, he placed the money in his small piggy bank and jumped back under his sheets.

Jabari cut off his light and opened the bedroom door to head over to his room. Before he could close it, Brandon raised his head. "Jabari?" he whispered.

"Wassup?"

"I love you."

He couldn't help but to smile as his little mini me crawled back under the sheets. "I love you too, champ," he whispered before closing his door lightly.

Creeping smoothly pass his dad's room, he could see the old man knocked out on his bed. It was one in the morning, which meant that he was surely gonna be up in a cool three hours to prepare for work. That was just enough time to get his thoughts together and prepare for school.

Walking inside his room, he closed the door and locked it. Throwing the money on his bed, he placed the gun under his pillow and sat down. Exhaling, he thought about the woman he killed and the bloody image of her flashed quickly through his eyes. It was a weird feeling, but what happened damn sure couldn't be changed. It was a part of the game, but he was damn sure glad that he didn't have to overload the way Keyno and Blow did. Killing wasn't on his agenda, only getting the funds to provide for the little one.

After counting up the paper, he placed it into the bottom of his dresser and decided to get some rest before the school day presented itself.

Chapter 2

Hagginwood - Sacramento, California

The ringing of Jabari's old alarm clock sounded just as his father entered the room. His old ass was never completely honest. He was never a perfect father either, but at the end, he was the only parent the boys had at the time. His smooth but old spirit always reminded everyone of an Isley Brother. He just knew he could sing a girl clean out her panties back in the day. Cali was only his stomping ground. A life back in the day where niggas dreamed of reigning king in Sacramento. That ambitious and tasty vision was his secret. It ended up falling when he decided to pick up his guns and take what he wanted.

"Jabari, the resting hours in the house is over, son. You should be up, and my damn sight should be on the back of yo small head walking out my front door. Yo brother is gone already. You betta get up out my house," he said in a pushy tone.

He was already bugging, and school didn't start until nine for Jabari anyway. Instead of ignoring him. He rolled over. "Dang Robert. It's seven in the morning. My bus don't even come until eight." Jabari placed his feet on the floor to wake up fully.

"I wouldn't give a damn if it didn't come 'til twelve a motherfuckin midnight, boy. Raise up or get blazed up." He held up his old ass fist as if he really still had it.

"I'm coming, man. I gotta get dressed, old fart."

"This fart a leave ya ass stanking and knocked the fuck out if you don't tighten up. You know the semester is almost over, and I'm proud of you, son. You actually get to do something I never got the chance to." Robert's dark

19

brown eyes beamed with passion while speaking his peace. Spending most of his childhood behind a wall was the cause of him not walking across stage, but it damn sure wasn't about to be his boys the same mistake.

"I know dad. Seven months, and it's over. I'm ready for it too. I'll be gone in ten minutes." He yawned and headed for the shower.

"Have a great day, Champ!" Robert said before closing the door so he could rush off to work.

The one thing Jabari knew, you couldn't be under Robert's household without going to school or having a damn job. He always said that shit. Even when he was in prison calling home for their mother. That nigga was the real dad from Friday the movie.

Jabari knew that every Individual within the bounds of this earth, explored, and released their mind in ways that many wouldn't understand. It's the reason everyone got created differently. Robert was just that Dad who didn't wanna hear excuses, cause that shit led to acceptance of just not giving a fuck. He wanted his boys stronger than the world could ever imagine. He didn't go a day without showing, and coaching the way.

After showering and tossing a leftover biscuit in the microwave, He locked up the house and headed out for school. Stepping out into the yard. He exhaled. The sun was shining bright like the first day of summer, and it felt like it was gonna take forever to end already. Heading for his bus stop. It arrived at a precise time, and scooped Jabari up for the same twenty-five-minute ride he took on a daily basis. Sliding the Beats headphones. He rested his eyes until it arrived

* * *

C. K. McClatchy High School

"Hold up, hold up, lil mama! What the hell do you think you're doing?" Teddy pulled up on a girl with his wallet out like a badge. "F. B. I. I'm a part of the Fine Body Investigators, and you playing the role in here with them lil bitty ass shorts." He smiled.

"Teddy, get yo dumb self away from me. You know it's a requirement of having money to talk to me," she fired back.

Teddy laughed. "See, I could have sat you on my cereal spoon and sucked ya down like some Apple Jacks, but your loss." He rubbed his hands together with a silly as grin.

The group of girls who were standing with her giggled.

The sound of Jabari's slow ass bus pulling in caused him to snap back to serious mode. After getting a text from Jabari about needing to talk, Teddy wanted to be the first to know and put his opinion on some shit.

Waiting patiently until he stepped off the bus, Teddy walked over to him with a curious eye like the Joker on "Batman". "Wassup with that secret doe?"

Jabari couldn't help but laugh. "Nigga, it's not a secret. It's just an idea. Calm down until we see the guys," he said before embracing him with a fist pound.

"Cool.

"When the hell you start getting to school so early anyway?"

"After all these fast ass girls start wearing all these tights, and Daisy Dukie damn shorts. That shit ain't just invisible around this motherfucker."

Jabari laughed at Teddy knowing that he was pass crazy. He was a friend ever since they stepped into McClatchy four years ago. He was always the "Mac" type fool. A playboy who couldn't be told no. His mind was one tracked unless he was somewhere playing football on the field. Teddy was the best when it came to running that ball. Standing at 5'8", he was built with a compact body, knocking shit clean over. If he didn't have a brush in his hands, he had a pen to write down another chick's number. Teddy's low haircut was always neat and his clothes was always the Thuggish Ruggish Bone look. A pair of sneakers, one long, crispy ass T shirt, and pair of khaki pants that was creased to the max.

"You gotta try not seeing most of this shit, bro. It really needs to be invisible. A girl's mind only pollutes you to lose track of the end goal. If you ain't finna marry her, then keep it pushing."

"Come on Jabari. I'm just doing what I was blessed to do. These girls need a big young nigga like me who can smother those porkchops. I'm just not leaving no gravy, cause I ain't taking care of no lil ones. Periodddd!" Teddy laughed.

"And that's ya problem right there."

Heading off into the school, the two of them made their way to the breakfast hall where another one of Jabari's friends pushed up with the quickness. Steven pushed his way through the crowded breakfast line and stopped in front of Jabari and Teddy. "Guys, I've been thinking. The new *Call of Duty* is to be preordered before its release date and I'm not trying to be the last one to suffer the fate of not receiving mines."

Teddy looked him up and down with a pathetic expression. "Steven, I'm quite sure you're the only friend of ours who still wears Hollister and American Eagle. Your damn collar shirt is about to suffocate you, man. Release the top button off ya neck, crazy."

Jabari laughed and patted his friends back. "It's alright, Steven. This nigga ain't use to preppy clothes and white man style things. He still got that broke man's mentality."

"Actually, my mother bought this for me. My father is seventy-five percent white, so he only wants the smooth fabrics of Gucci and Giovanni; whatever that is." Steven brushed off the comment and removed his cellphone.

"Jabari, what do you think about this? An article about marijuana says that we can build a billion-dollar weed farm in the bounds of Colorado within three year if we have the right materials and foundation."

"Weed? Colorado? Steven, this is California. We can do that here."

"But not everywhere. This is Sacramento. We need space like Colorado to expand and have the legitimacy of selling what we please."

"Maybe. It's not where I'm really at now though." Jabari grabbed his tray and headed for a table. Teddy and Steven followed.

Steven was one of the smart guys in the crew, but he was a true geek for all things like Comic Cons, and action figures. He felt that if the guys placed their mind into investments and businesses while their school foundation was going, they could probably be millionaires by the time college crept around. Unfortunately, none of the guys wanted to be a smart specialist like him when it came down to the worldly things of making money. They only wanted shit the easy way.

Steven was skinny framed built with glasses that looked like they could view the gases and chemicals that rested on Mars. Nothing could stop him from winning all the science fairs or contest in school, He was just naturally digging into anything that had shit to offer about learning new things in the world. That's what he was placed on earth for because he damn sure was good at it. Most people would pick on him and try little small shit to embarrass him some days. That was until Jabari decided to end the bullshit. He and Steven had been friends since elementary school. If there was a problem where anybody wanted to escalate with violence towards Steven, he would gladly be the one to bite it. He didn't bar none when it came to the ones that he cared about, plus the small Karate classes Jabari was enrolled in at the age of ten did major justice for him. He was a black belt in Wing Chun, and Brazilian Jujitsu. That alone allowed him major respect behind the walls of McClatchy High school. Nobody wanted to go against that, especially the ones who knew him personally. In the mix of the conversation.

Leo's large frame leaned over both of their shoulders. "What y'all shrimps talking about?" He grabbed an apple off Jabari's tray and bit it.

He was another friend of Jabari's since the sandbox. He was 6'2" with a slim body. Probably slim enough to pick a keyhole. Leo was the last addition to the four-man bunch. He was the muscle man next to Jabari, and he surely didn't play when it came to breaking into some shit on that damn laptop. Hacking that is.

"Wassup with it? What's new?" Jabari asked as he munched on the small breakfast.

"A whole lot. I found a way to shut off the school lights by tapping into the main electricity box in the security room."

"That's lit. What about the girls bathroom?" Teddy stuck his tongue out with a stupid grin.

"Hell nah. Not unless you wanna go to prison and be a nigga's punching bag. You better leave these girls alone." Leo tapped a few keys on his laptop and killed all the lights inside the cafeteria.

The loud chatter rose after the darkness clouded the room. Once they flickered back on, Jabari smiled. "That's nice. You gotta see if you can upgrade to knocking an entire block out."

"Man listen, It's really nothing that I can't do on this bitch. I'm fucking the system and just tricking a few buttons around to make it do what I need. We can use this to our advantage when I learn how to really master it."

"That's good, but this is a serious conversation. I need all of y'all to listen up too." Jabari grabbed all of their attention quickly. The lunchroom was spread lost in a wave of stupidity with the minor things, so he wasn't worried about anyone eavesdropping on their talk.

Digging in his pocket, he pulled put six-thousand dollars wrapped in two thousand-dollar bundles. Passing all of them one, he continued to eat, but still kept his vision on them. Everyone held their silence looking at the cash. Steven was the smart one who examined it and placed it into his pocket without any questions. Leo made a scene counting his little change with a bright smile and Teddy flipped the damn rubber band off that bitch like he just hit the lottery. "Hold up, Jabari. Is this my college tuition or did you choke a bitch out for her stripper money? Nigga, this is two bands. Where did you get it?" He grinned.

Jabari shook his head before sliding the tray to the side. He realized that if he needed something done quietly, it was definitely going to be Steven handling the job. "I ran across something sweet and decided to see how y'all feel about it."

"Sweet like coochie or sweet like laptops with a nasty HD camera and a freaky ass entertainment surround sound?" Leo added on with a Teddy's dumb ass comment.

"Sweet like the laptop shit" Jabari laughed not trying to divert away from his serious questions.

"Sweeeettttttt," Teddy, and Leo sounded off at the same time.

"Would you clowns please listen." Jabari slapped his forehead with frustration. The only one who was sitting quietly was Steven, and he was always prepared to learn something new if it came down to helping all of them.

"Aite Go ahead Malcolm X," Teddy encouraged him before stuffing the paper into his pocket.

Jabari pointed a stern finger letting him know that he didn't take lightly on talking about the historical Black veterans. "Look dummy. Yesterday, I was thinking when I divided up this money in my room, well, really it was early this morning. We need a stable balance of how we're gonna be eating out here. The way I made this happen wasn't my preference, but it was decent enough for me to save some and come break y'all off two grand a piece," he announced before shrugging his shoulders.

"Okkkayyy, and we still waiting for you to tell us what the hell you did to make six grand or however much you got left because you damn sure didn't give us all of it," Leo said with a straight face.

"Heyyy, Jabari" a group of four girls said in unison, as they moved pass the table waving their fingers like a porn video was about to start.

"Hey," he mumbled, and turned back to his friends without even showing the slightest interest. "As I was saying. I made a move last night and it went smooth, but I'm thinking bigger."

"So basically, you went and laid a nigga ass down for the cheese and didn't invite me." Teddy smirked.

"Or me," Leo chimed in.

"It wasn't like that. I was with Keyno and Blow."

Once he mentioned their names, Teddy and Leo acted as if he trashed a pound of shit turds against their cafeteria table. No one really liked him to be around the grown ass killers, especially with the word that was going around town about the two of them.

"What?" Jabari watched as they both tooted their noses.

"I'm actually good without laying people down. You didn't have to tell me anything, Jabari. I'm quite sure you handled it very well," Steven added.

"Shut up dweeb," Teddy said before cutting his eyes back at Jabari. "Nigga, you know we don't deal with those fools. Them niggas are grown as fuck, and not to mention, they're killing people, not just taking," Teddy said seriously.

"Everybody isn't being murdered just because you hear the word robbing Teddy." Jabari folded his arms.

"Yea maybe, but when it comes down to Keyno and Blow, the word robbing means *Death Valley*, *The Chronicles of Riddick*, *Hostel*, and every other scary ass movie that I can think of where a motherfucker getting slaughtered. Them niggas are crazy."

"That's understandable, but those same crazy ass niggas made sure I was able to come across twenty grand last night."

Leo nearly leaned his tall ass body across the table to be sure he heard clearly. "Twenty what?"

"Twenty thousand dollars," Jabari said with a wry smile.

"Well that do sound reasonable to blast a bitch. Are them niggas taking applications?" 'Teddy's dumbass switched to go when he heard that shit.

The loud school bell sounded, signaling for them to get to their homerooms. Jabari looked around at all the teenagers moving about and stood to his feet. "We really need to talk, but school is important. Y'all need to ride the bus home instead of riding. This will help all of us."

"If you say so, Jabari. You know whatever you say is gold, my friend. After class." Leo tapped his shoulder and dispersed from the cafeteria.

"I'm with it. I don't give a damn what you got going on. You ain't been letting us down. Don't start now, Bari. You the champ. That's in yo dad's voice." Teddy made an old man's expression before rushing off.

Jabari laughed and looked over at Steven. "Let's get to homeroom class before we be late, man."

"Cool. But let me ask you something, Jabari. What is a dweeb? Because Teddy considers that I'm this thing within in our circle. Specifically, I know that it was short for dweebish, something like a nerd who suffers from wearing corny clothes."

Jabari shook his head and placed his arm around his best friend's neck. "Steven, don't even try figure it out. You're a dweeb, but you're my dweeb," he laughed.

Chapter 3

Hagginwood
Afterschool - 2:58P. M.

The bus pulled off leaving a trail of tar black smoke behind.

Teddy coughed and dusted the side of his Dickie khaki's. "See Jabari, this is why I don't take the bus when my dad has a raggedy ass car. Everybody don't like the hood, man."

Jabari moved with Steven across the street and Leo trailed along, tapping on his laptop as usual. "So, I'm saying. We did have a talk that needed to be established, right?"

"Yes. Money is what I needed to talk to you all about. We're all broke. None of us are fortunate enough to keep pushing through this poverty ass mind state if we don't step up. I laid down some shit last night, but I don't wanna keep robbing people."

"Well, in that case, you might as well stop robbing people all around because it's gonna be somebody involved in every robbery, Jabari. We rob niggas. That's what we do," Teddy said with fake ass mug knowing he ain't never took shit in his life but an ass beating.

"Nah fool, I've been taking my chances, but besides that one store, you ain't robbed shit. I wanna feed Brandon, man. My dad's a fucking maintenance man who mops at a private school. My mom is on crack. I don't have no other choice but to get some money."

"So, what are you talking about?" Leo closed his laptop and joined in the mix.

Jabari looked over at Steven before he spoke, "Banks."

"Banks? You mean like ski mask, *Set it Off* shit. Banks?" Leo grinned.

"Exactly." Jabari nodded.

"What the hell makes ya think you ready to do some dumb shit like that?" Teddy stopped in the street and looked at them all.

"What makes you think we aren't? We've did these petty ass moves terrorizing our neighborhood when we should be taking it back from the government. I'm tired of hurting black people. I want the white-collar money."

"Actually, banks is one of the least crimes committed in Sacramento. It's only a few banks around this way that carries more than seventy-five grand in the front counters. A four to five-man job will get you something bigger like the River City Bank over on 912th Street."

"And how do you know this?" Leo second guessed Steven's statement.

"Because. My mom's husband works for a national bank out in Los Angeles. He does finances for over thirty different banks worldwide, and most of the ones in Sacramento aren't that different. They're actually similar," He assured Jabari with a thumbs up.

The thought of stepping it up was eating at his flesh. He didn't want to be living in the shadows of Hagginwood learning the legacy of a basic hood nigga. He really wanted the fast way out.

"Don't you think we would have to take notes on all this?"

"I can get the routes of the bank and see if I can trigger their alarm. It'll probably work for like twenty-five to forty seconds though. I told you that I've been working," Leo added.

"Sounds like we got a master plan, but we have to get Keyno and Blow to hear out that proposition," Jabari said as they headed down through the neighborhood.

People moved about freely and the sun was beaming on every corner. Even though it seemed to be so sweet, Hagginwood was one of the most dangerous sections in Sacramento. It was largely populated balance in the area when it involved murder. There was other sections like Old Sacramento. That's where Teddy was born and raised, but recently moved out to Hagginwood after his mother died. Leo was from Ben Ali. It was nothing but rough ass neighborhoods in the vicinity of their city. Through it all, Jabari refused to let the streets choose him to be a statistic. Standing 5'11" with a medium athletic build, Jabari could easily move some shit out his way. His brown, curly hair was a shade darker than his tan, brown skin. His eyes were a gift from god. His stare alone could make a woman cringe. Jabari was humble from head to toe. He was never the type to feed off a woman. Standing on finding a righteous queen was instilled in his mind, and he wasn't about to settle for just anything.

As the boys walked deeper into the hood, the sound of Blow's Jeep Cherokee engine was like a Lamborghini's engine roaring and sliding across the concrete. The twelve-inch speakers and sub woofers in his trunk was whamming louder than a swole midget stuck in a trash can. His shit always quaked through the hood, waking everybody up out they sleep and shit. It really was his pleasure to piss people off and make everyone hate him because he didn't give a damn how a motherfucker felt. Blow was twenty years old. Only three years older than Jabari, but his lifestyle was a wild one. He already had five murders under his belt, and was no telling on how many people the nigga had laid down since he'd been around Keyno. Blow was already draped in some fly shit. Nothing casual, only street gear. His long hair was able to let him jump in between most of the thirsty women's legs who was around the area. If it wasn't taking a niggas money, it was him slaying another man's chick. The point was simple. Blow was that guy that no one truly likes, but they deal with him in order to keep him calm in a certain sense.

Blow didn't hesitate to pull down on their small group once he saw them enter the neighborhood. Stopping his four-door Jeep in the street, he rolled down his window and called Jabari and his crew to the car. "Yo lil nigga. Y'all come here real quick." He waved his hand like of was some important shit.

All four of them made their way over and looked into the window. Blow inhaled on a giant blunt of weed while playing with an exquisite assault rifle in his hands. He smiled once he noticed the young one's attention was on him. "If any of y'all can tell what type of gun this is, I'll give you a hundred dollars," he bluffed, pointing at the bankroll on his front seat.

Everybody tried their best to guess, but Steven didn't hesitate. "That's an H&K 48 Automatic. It holds a fifty round magazine and supposed to have a red beam installed directly on the side of the barrel." He pointed at Blow's gun wit assurance.

The crew grew quiet not knowing if their friend was accurate. Blow stepped out of the car and looked him up and down. "How the fuck you know that? Let me guess. Ya dad is a police officer?" He laughed with the gun still in his hands

"No, those same guns are actually on Call of Duty. The recoil on it is horrible, and it's a horrible gun if you were really trying to harm someone. You would probably make one shot out of ten depending on what's your target." Steven looked down at the big piece of metal.

It's like Blow's anger triggered out of nowhere, or he thought that Steven was being funny, because the crew couldn't get out a good laugh before he raised the gun to Steven's face. "How about we test it out now?" Blow grinned with his fingers inside the trigger hole.

Jabari wasted no time stepping up behind him. His laughing face was completely gone. "Blow, get that gun out of his face!"

Steven trembled lightly and closed his eyes. He was never the type to buck or fight, which was the reason Jabari stepped in. Blow ignored his command until he moved Steven himself and stepped in front of the gun. "I said stop playing and lower that gun, nigga. You can't fucking hear?" Jabari questioned with bass in his voice.

Blow laughed before tightening his hand around the handle and trigger. "Who gonna stop me, lil nigga?"

His friends could see the situation escalating, and Leo reached over to grab Jabari's arm. "Bro, let's just go. Leave it alone."

"Fuck that. He ain't about to do shit." Jabari moved Leo's arm and continued to stare him down. "I don't know who the fuck you think we are, nigga, but being a bitch ain't in my blood. That's my second time telling you that," Jabari barked without blinking.

The sight of Keyno's 2017 Cadillac escalade pulling down forced Blow to lower his strap with a smile. "Damn lil nigga. It was just a joke. Be easy hothead."

Keyno's truck came to a smooth halt, and the driver's window rolled down. "What's good? Why you out here being stupid, my nigga? I saw you from way up the street, Blow. Put that shit the fuck up!" he ordered aggressively.

"It was a joke, Keyno. You know I ain't about to shoot these little niggas."

"I said put it up. Now!"

Blow tooted up his nose at Jabari and the rest of his little crew. "Damn, now I can't bust a move with y'all rats. Y'all a let a nigga get jammed I see," he fussed before jumping back into the driver's seat of his Jeep.

Teddy kicked his foot in the air once Blow smashed off. "Man, I hate that nigga. Somebody let me pop his stupid ass."

"Man, you wasn't about to do shit. I was cutting my eyes the entire time at you fool." Jabari waved off his threat.

Keyno couldn't help but to laugh when he looked at the way Jabari carried himself. He reminded him so much of his own childhood that it was scary. That was the reason Keyno introduced him on how to really get money. It wasn't the correct way, but it was damn sure the easiest when you knew how to stick and move without even leaving a trace. It was knowledge Keyno continued to mold on him until he mastered the art of clocking the jack game precisely. "Jabari, come here for a second young one. All y'all come here, matter fact." He waved over Leo, Steven, and Teddy also.

The young twelfth graders crowded around Keyno's truck as if they were about receive one of the best lectures a preacher had to offer to a recovering addict. "I see y'all everyday together. This four-man squad is all y'all need. I've been knowing y'all since ya first start crossing the streets by yaself, and I applaud y'all for sticking together through the years, but what's next? I keep hearing y'all want money and need college funds paid for, but that shit don't come easy."

"We're thinking about that too, Keyno," Jabari answered for all of them.

"You ain't gotta think when you got me on your team. You say you want money, I'll give you the licks and y'all cut me a percentage after its done. Now, whatever y'all find on the money tip is automatic split, but whatever else in that bitch is good for the taking. I don't wanna be to frank, but y'all crew look like a gun ain't even in you niggas' vocabulary."

"Looks can be deceiving," Leo said with arrogance.

Teddy and Steven remained quiet, but Jabari didn't want to miss his chance and what needed to be said. "We wanna hit a bank."

"A bank?" Keyno cracked a small laugh. "You must be watching too many movies, Jabari. That ain't just a simple task."

"I know that we can do it. You just have to supply me with some bigger guns. It's more profitable than running in some black family's home and taking what they worked hard for. Taking is taking, Keyno." Jabari folded his arms.

Keyno smiled before peeling him off eight hundred-dollar bills. "Look, go buy all of y'all a throw away phone. No one should have the numbers but the group, meaning you four. I'm feeling what you saying about the bank thing. I'd rather see how the smaller missions go first and I'll let you know if y'all ready to make that step. Trust me." He pointed at the dog tag that was dangling on Jabari's neck

"I know Keyno. Man, stop second guessing me." He gave Keyno a pound and walked off with Teddy, Steven, and Leo following.

"So, what now? We still robbing houses or nah?" Teddy asked with a curious face.

"Until Keyno say it's a go, we will do this with them. But remember, they think that I've only did one lick in my entire life. They don't know about our movement. We ain't hurting nobody. If a gun gets pulled, it'll be from whoever we laying down, disobeying the orders. If our hands are forced, then cool. Besides that, we need to show him that we can operate without hurting anyone like they're used to doing."

"That's easy. You know the number one rule." Leo looked at Teddy with a straight face.

"Don't Panic," they all said in unison.

Cracking a small laugh, Jabari placed the money into Leo's hand. "The electronic store is right beside yo hood, nigga. Grab us all a throw away like Keyno said. Whatever we discuss is between us. This is our way out of here bro."

"Cut the sad talk and get focused. We got this. No gay shit between the boys," Teddy laughed while walking the opposite way with Leo.

Jabari flicked him a bird and headed down his street with Steven directly beside him. Before he could even ask Steven's opinion on what Keyno offered, his mother, Mrs. Morgan, stepped out on her porch and called his name, "Steveenn! Let's go. I'm pretty sure you have homework, honey. Good evening Jabari." She waved lightly.

"Well, I guess this is why he wants us to get cells. She just cut into the conversation like a bad wireless service. See ya later, brother." He patted Jabari's back before dashing off towards his home. Mrs. Morgan wasn't the average mom when it came down to him. Regardless of Steven being seventeen, she knew that he could be easily manipulated. Of course, she knew Jabari was a dear friend, but the bounds of Sacramento wasn't going to be the downfall of her offspring.

Jabari walked into the and yard and went inside to prepare for the daily Tuesday meal. Fried chicken patties, sweet peas out the can, and a batch of Pillsbury Doughboy biscuits. One of the most decent meals throughout the week in their household.

Jabari Gunz was born on a cold winter night. He knew that life wasn't sweet considering the family's shortcomings with money. Instead of sitting around when he was younger, he tried to go and make it however possible. His little brother, Brandon, was just a casualty in the disturbing way they were raised. You had certain people who would get it by any means when it came down to feeding their kids, and then you had lazy individuals who felt that shit wasn't gonna get better unless they hit the lottery or something.

Their mother, Tanya Gunz, was the apple that fell forty miles from her tree in order for this to occur. See, a pimp and a hoe in one household could never work, especially when that pimp and hoe was their father and mom. Fights would happen at the worse times and there was never any time to be a true family when getting along was never a part of their goals and mission. After Ronald left when Jabari was two years old, it placed the household into his mom's hands and that was one of the hardest times Jabari ever experienced in his life.

Their mother was addicted to crack for a long period of time, but the crazy shit was, no one knew about it until Ronald left to do his time. Tanya was always the go out and get her money type of chick. She didn't need a nigga slapping a hand across her head in order to move and make something happen. The lifestyle of her smoking dope fell from the sky when their dad happened to take his fall. Throughout their entire life, Jabari never knew the story on how Tanya changed for the worse. All he knew is that his mom needed help, and before he let his brother settle with nothing, he would go and snatch whatever he could to contribute. That stern way of thinking stuck with him as he grew older in the Hagginwood area. It was nothing else to do but get into some shit and learn how to survive in the midst of hard times and suffering.

After Jabari pulled all the necessary ingredients out for his father to prepare dinner, his little brother was speeding through the door with the quickness. "Did you get it? What do my clothes look like?" he was asking questions and looking around for any sign of his new gear to show off in his school.

Jabari grabbed his shoulder. "Calm down. I haven't got it yet? All you need to do is focus and remember to keep this secret between me and you until I can tell dad where I came up on this amount of cash. Remember?"

"Yeah, yeah, I remember. I don't see what the big deal is Bari. People get new clothes all the time. I'm like the only kid in middle who's trucking around in some tacky old gear. Dad should be happy you buying me something new. Them thrift clothes smell like an old lady's basement. I'm tired of wearing that shit."

"Aye, watch ya mouth lil one. I don't need you picking up on no bad habits around here." He pointed a finger to let his little brother know that he wasn't playing.

Brandon lowered his head, feeling the catastrophe of their life was the only light he could see. Jabari touched his shoulder. "Listen, lil one. I know you think that things will never change. It feels surreal sometimes, but we will make it through this. I was always hoping that one day we could just wake up and be straight. I mean straight enough to where we don't gotta worry, but we're not there yet."

"Why do we gotta suffer? How come all these other people can have these big houses and clean clothes, but we eating hotdogs and chips for dinner every night? I wanna live better, Jabari. Not just to eat a good dinner but live better with all the things we do. We deserve that," he stressed folding his arms.

"You're right, but that doesn't mean anything without keeping faith lil one. We have to pray and ask for guidance because all the shit I'm doing isn't correct either. I do it because I know that you need certain stuff, and you're getting older. Just cause you feel like I'm taking money, doesn't mean that doesn't come with consequences, Brandon."

"I understand," he huffed, not wanting to hear the Black Power lectures Jabari always tossed on him. It was all overboard on his young mind. Those type of things didn't matter when you were in a new time and age inside the world.

Jabari play punched him. "In the morning, I promise to go out and get you new clothes. I don't give a damn what pop says. I know you haven't had anything new all school year, so don't give up on me just yet. Trust me."

"I trust you, Jabari. I don't have no choice, remember?" he mocked him sarcastically.

"You better know it." He smiled at his little brother before mushing his head lightly. "Now, go and tackle the little homework you got so we can get on some of this *Fight Night Round Three,* punk."

Brandon grabbed his bookbag with a wide grin. "Boy, it's on. I just learned how to play with Ali, so can't nobody beat me."

"Well, we about to see. I don't wanna hear all that. I'm getting Holyfield and knocking something out, champ." He balled up his fist and placed it up to Brandon's eye.

The two brothers shared a laugh before he left Jabari in the kitchen to handle his cooking duties. Their father usually was the one to take care of preparing the food, but late days where he pulled over time, left the responsibility in the hands of his oldest.

A few hours passed, and within that time Jabari kicked Brandon's butt in the game over thirty times. His chores of sweeping the back porch and taking care of the trash was done. And last but not least, he was able to get some studying in out of the Huey P. Newton biography. Jabari was very farfetched when it came to applying his mind to understanding novels like the one, he was entangled in. A lot of studies on Black history interested him because of the way the Black's had changed drastically since the time where the legends applied their life to help them all.

Ronald walking through the front door snapped him out of the book trance. "Champ, how's it going?" He sat down his bag and toolbox.

Jabari continued to read the last few words of the chapter before placing the book down on the kitchen table. "Wassup, Ronald?"

"My name is Dad, not Ronald, Jabari. Show some respect." He headed for the kitchen sink and washed his hands. "Did you prepare dinner?"

"Yeah. It's been ready for the past hour. Glad you was able to make it before the roaches decided to have a feast."

"Very funny. Where's your brother?"

"Brandon! It's time to eat, lil one. Let's make it happen," Jabari yelled out before taking his seat at the kitchen table.

Ronald grabbed three glass plates out of the cabinet and placed them on the table where the food was already set up nicely. "So, how was school? Did you ask the teacher about how those school fees can be lowered?"

"Yeah. She said it's impossible."

"Impossible? Well that's gonna be a problem because I don't make enough to pay the bills, and support school bills also. They making up all types of things now. Stuff like this wasn't going on when we were enrolled in our classes."

"Dad. That was almost thirty-seven years ago. School don't even remember the things you guys were learning. It's too old for anyone to remember in that case," Jabari laughed.

"Boy, let me tell you something. Back then, I was the man. The teachers would've probably wrote me a pass that said you're fine and don't have to do ya homework. I was the main attraction in my class." Ronald smiled as if he was a young playa heading for the nearest basketball game with his little chick.

Brandon walked into the kitchen and sat down in his chair. Without speaking to his father, he grabbed a biscuit and began to naw on that bitch like it was the last supper.

Jabari looked at him as if he just signed a death certificate for himself.

Ronald grabbed a napkin and placed it on his lap. "Sit the bread down until we say grace boy. You don't respect the family rules anymore?" he questioned with a raised eye.

Jabari smiled before bowing his head and closing his eyes. He knew his little brother was a beast when it came down to listening, but who could blame a child that was living with a father he only known for a year and some change.

Ronald quickly bowed his head and blessed the food. Once the boys began to eat, he looked over at Jabari who was still reading the biography of his mentor. "Son, don't you think that can wait until after you finish eating?"

"Nah. Learning is important, dad. The school definitely ain't gonna teach me this right here," he said, before biting one of the chicken patties on his plate.

"Well, what in the hell do y'all learn in that school up there?"

"Whatever the teachers want us to learn. That's the basic slave minded stuff those people teach. You know, like the Bill of Rights, the U. S Constitution, and how that fake guy, Christopher Columbus, discovered America. It's the normal bull stuff the parents love for their children to be fed in the school district."

"There is no such thing as bull in school, boy. All of it is history, no matter how you look at it. It may not be the shit that you wanna hear like the rising of Negros and the killing with the worthless nonsense of how the people abandoned laws because of their own choices. I used to be the same way, and that shit ended up costing me nearly my whole life behind a wall."

"Yeah. That's the part I'm not trying to know, dad. Seems like our people stood for something different and not just accepting the treatment of a person who don't care for our kind. I would rather stand on my own before I work a slave job for the man."

Brandon nudged Jabari's foot under the table.

Ronald took a spoonful of sweet peas into his mouth before sitting down his fork. "What's wrong with a job?

What in the hell makes it a slave job, if you don't mind me asking?

"I didn't mean it like that, Pop." Jabari regretted making the low statement. It was hard to accept that he was one of those critical mind thinkers who depended on the government for a way to live. It was kind of pathetic because at the mind of seventeen, Jabari wanted to have more and it damn sure wasn't gonna come from working hard in another man's empire.

"Nah, I wanna hear this. What makes you think that the shit parents get out here to do every day is a slave job. It puts clothes on y'all backs. Maybe not the ones you want, but some to keep you warm. Including this home. This food. It don't seem like a slave house if you eating off glass plates that I bought. So, tell me what you mean about a slave. I guess that makes me one too, huh?" Ronald took a sip of his tea and rested his cup back on the table.

Jabari knew that his father didn't like the fact of being tested by his knowledge. Neither did he like to feel like a worthless ass father under his own roof. It was a debate that happened often between the two, but it never stopped Jabari from keeping it uncut with him. "Yes, in reality, it's a slave man's job, dad. You making minimum wages, mopping floors and cleaning for the same people who call us monkeys and niggas. Nine dollars an hour to put up with something a kid can do at the age of seven on up. I don't wanna spend my whole life going to school and still end up doing something like that for the rest of my life."

"So what's better, Jabari? Sneaking around with those fake ass gangstas you hang with? Them idiots are gonna get ya ass a life sentence. How much do they pay you in the prison system? It damn sure ain't gonna be what I make, cause you'll be doing that shit for free. Extra trays, and snacks will get ya throat slit in two like a bitch busting her legs open with her period still on. I'll wait for you to tell me which one sounds better." Ronald placed a hand under his chin.

"Nothing. I was just referring to myself, dad. I don't wanna be doing that for the rest of my life. It's hard hearing the truth, but that's the reality for me, Pop. I refuse to sign myself over to these people."

"Treasure is found in some of the dirtiest water, Jabari. Just because I work somewhere that you may not, doesn't mean that no one else isn't willing to kill for that job. Certain people out there can't even take care of their families because of no damn work. I would be glad if I was shoveling shit in order to feed the ones that I love." He scooped up his plate and walked off from the kitchen table.

Brandon sat quietly finishing his food until Ronald headed to the back for his room. Looking over at Jabari, he shook his head. "You know that he's not ready to deal with that genius side of your mind. Those things have to be taken slow when you're dealing with an old man like dad."

"I see. I'm sorry for being the bad guy, but that's the truth. I'm not gonna hide the way I feel just because he screwed up his life. That's not my fault."

"Yeah, but he's our dad, Jabari."

"Cool. I'm glad you feel like that. You should be able to handle the thrift store ass clothes he buying you then. The point of me saying something was to let him know that I have a mind of my own, Brandon. It wasn't to belittle him or make fun of what he does for a living. It's sad, but it's true. That one maintenance job will not feed us for the rest of our lives, let alone his own," Jabari said before rising from his seat. Tossing the plate inside of the sink, he grabbed his book and headed out of the back door.

Jabari knew that some days was better than the most, but the reality of them being poor set in more every day. Just not too long ago, he could remember their mom coming back to her senses from the poison she was using. Happy days were rare within their little circle, but there was nothing like that mama love to keep a better spirit floating around the atmosphere. Regardless of how bad things may looked, she was true to making sure they understood what family meant. The thought of losing them pained her, but the addiction just couldn't shake away.

Using the ladder to head up on the roof, Jabari stepped up and exhaled once he got to the top. The dark crystal stars danced around in the sky as if it was time to introduce a famous entertainer for a daily night of classic comedy. It was strange when he viewed the world for what it truly was within the future. Each year more stars would disappear. There used to be a time where you could come and sit outside to see the stars move around swiftly as if you could pick them off the sky's boarder with your fingertips. Now, you come out and barely could see a bundle of enough stars to form the big dipper.

Jabari pulled a rolled joint from his pocket and used his small lighter to spark it up. Inhaling on the good marijuana, he nearly choked after Leo's tall ass scared him to death. The nigga was already 6'2", so it was quite easy for him to step on the ladder and look up on the small ass roof. A few steps was all it took and he was walking on the thin ass installation towards Jabari.

"I see somebody don't know how to answer the damn phone. I guess it's no point of you needing this." Leo flashed the throwaway touchscreen phone.

Jabari nodded with smile. "I see you don't waste no time. Somebody is really trying to get some money," he said before Leo took a seat next to him.

"So wassup? You on top of the roof and you only come up here when you in yo feelings. What happened now?"

Jabari couldn't do nothing but exhale from the comment. It was sad that his friends knew when something wasn't going right inside the household. It was like a mirror with a dirty reflection that you couldn't hide. The bond between him and Ronald was horrible some days. It was like he didn't even exist within his father's world. Their mind frames were on two different levels, and the way he felt about the society was the same shit that Ronald when to prison and stood on.

"I'm beefing with my dad about the same shit. He wants to be slave minded and I wanna be free. I can't blame the fact that I grew up with a surrounding to stand up instead of laying down. He committed all types of crimes back in the day just to switch up and kiss the people's ass who tried to take him away." Jabari shook his head with a pathetic expression.

"You gotta understand, Jabari. Everybody not gonna have the mind that you do, neither will everybody have the heart that you possess. You a different type of breed, bro. I'm not saying that just because we been friends forever. You got a voice Jabari, but that doesn't mean that all the people will stand up and listen," Leo said, trying to break his saggy spirit. He knew once Jabari was in the phase, he could shut down and start to close everyone out. It wasn't fair, but that's just the way he dealt with the world. He felt that solitary space was better in order to find peace, and balance within the mind. The one thing that he wouldn't change was his drive for that money. It was his natural motto to get paper, and Ronald wasn't going to stop that no matter what he tried to preach.

"I'm thinking bigger than just the projects, Leo. I want power, money, and the respect. I want us to live without worry of anyone touching this crew. A true King in this city who don't work for nobody."

"Yeah, but everybody gotta work with someone in order to achieve that level. You can't do it by yourself, my dude." Leo embraced him with a hug and brotherly handshake.

"Word," Jabari mumbled as he continued to stare out at the night sky.

Leo left quickly as he came and allowed Jabari to have his personal space. Not too many wanted to see the boy when he was mad. His attitude was beyond horrible, and it was hard to calm him down. Most would say that it was his rebelliousness with Ronald, but it was more than that. Jabari was a leader. He refused to follow a man who didn't have enough courage to fight for himself and his family on top of that. One thing he knew for sure. Whatever was meant to happen upon this journey he was about to embark on. He knew that it would be the path he was bound to endure.

Chris Green

Chapter 4

6:45 A.M.

It had been six hours ago when Jabari popped the first movie in about a team on their bank robbing sprees. It was called "Heat", and the men was more than just professionals when it came to tackling a safe. It was more than just one way to skin a cat and money wasn't only inside of the banks either. The film literally gave him small details on shit that he would need to break down with his crew. It was obvious that security would be strapped, so stepping in that bitch would require the muscle who wouldn't be scared to pop their gun. The alarm systems would probably be a small button near the counter drawer of the employees. It was easy access in case a robber came in. That was another problem they would surely have to worry about. All Jabari wanted to do was calculate shit down to a T. If he didn't get anything right, he knew that earning his family a check would be a story to speak about. It had no choice, but to go as planned when the mastermind was doing all the plotting.

Ronald walking inside the room grabbed Jabari's attention. He looked down at the notepad in his hand and realized that he was obviously on another Black Power rampage. Being that it was too early, he changed this thoughts and asked simple question, "It's six in the morning and you're up looking at bank robbery movies. School is at nine, are you gonna be ready?"

"I'm already up ain't it, Ronald?" Jabari looked down at all his clothes as if he was fully dressed for nothing

You could tell that he wanted to bite the smart ass comment, but instead, he allowed it to pass. "Listen boy, be out my house at 8:00 A. M. I wouldn't give a damn what you got going on." He slammed the door and headed out of the house for work.

After waiting a cool ten minutes for Ronald to get away from the crib, Jabari grabbed his Jordan string book bag and headed out. Five-thousand dollars was in his pocket and the throw away cell phone Keyno asked them to grab yesterday was already activated. His mission was simple.

Today was to check out a few things for his brother at Arden Fair Mall and drop by at the West Armor Bank down on Arden Way. The walk wasn't long, and by the time he trucked for a cool thirty minutes, he reached the destination of the bank and stood across the street. Certain cars had just begun to come in and Jabari decided to smoke a joint while he waited. Rolling up a small doobie, he dug in his pocket for a lighter to spark it, but the armored truck that turned inside the bank's driveway caused him to pause. The sight of one officer stepping out the driver seat forced him to pay attention.

A second guard stepped out of the passenger with his gun in hand, as if he was elected to hire the President. The set up was definitely pretty stupid because one officer stayed outside and the other went inside to conduct whatever business was at hand. Looking at the time in his cell, it was 8:47 a.m. The streets were slightly dry and it started to make sense that these slow ass officers were trying to pick up a load of whatever was walking out of the building in the officer's right hand. A medium size bag was in his grasp and he was being more than careful as he headed back for the truck. The guarding officer made sure the back door was opened so they could secure whatever amount of paper that was contained in the bag. That's when Jabari spotted the third officer who held a shotgun in his palms. Once he grabbed the bag, the door was shut back and the two officers retreated back inside the truck. If three men would've been on point with Jabari, That move could have happened right then and there. It was common sense that if one officer was shot or hurt in any manner, the other assholes would comply. It was always a difference when you were prepared to murder someone in order to receive that payday. When Jabari noticed a car pull inside the lot and park, he watched a man climb from the whip and make his way into the building. That was his chance to move and be quick.

Dashing across the street, Jabari made his way slowly into the parking lot of the West Armor Bank without second guessing. He walked inside the double door facility, and his eyes instantly landed on the guard who stood stiffer than a damn mime. A large pistol rested on his hip and his eyes rotated over to Jabari before he could move. "Is there something you need help with sir?"

"Yes, I'm trying to see how to open up a line of credit a with this bank. It's hard for me to take care of my brother with the catastrophes going on with the jobs around here. The fraud is off the charts and I'm not trying to lose the little money that I do have," Jabari said pulling out the five-thousand dollars that rested in his pocket.

"No problem, sir. Just step over to that young lady at the front desk and she'll be able to help you with whatever you need," he answered sternly.

"Thanks." Jabari flashed a fake smile and headed directly over to the woman. It was always easier to deal with a woman instead of a man when it came down to issues like money, especially money that was about to be taken. Strolling over to the front desk, she looked up into Jabari's face and gave him a small wink.

"Hello, young man. Can I help you?" Her posture loosened up like she was offering him a place to stay for the night.

"Uh yeah. I was wondering if I wanted to start a bank account, which would be the best one to open. I heard this bank is good for business and I'm not trying to lose out on my money," He repeated again before flashing her the money.

"Of course, I'll be able to help you. There are different bank accounts we can open today. I'll just grab some paperwork for you, handsome, and we can get started," she mumbled flirtatiously.

"Thanks," Jabari said, looking at everything else but her ass. She was a nice healthy white woman and her butt was bigger than he expected it to be when she stood. It caused him to double take and even pay her a small amount of attention. That thang was moving like a melted Jell-O cup in her black suit pants. Her hair was blonde with a long black ribbon tying it down. Her blouse was slightly open, giving Jabari a full sight of her cleavage that was dying for attention. By the time she arrived back to the table, he already peeped out all of the things he needed. The bank teller slid a paper closer to him. "Sign this and we can get started."

"Cool," he said, quickly reading over the paper like that shit was really important.

"How old are you?" She made a curious grin.

"I'm eighteen and a half." He winked before placing his attention back on the papers in front of him. By the time he was done filling out the necessary forms to start an account, she was sliding him another paper with her phone number attached.

"My name is Sarah. You can call me personally if you need any assistance on learning the avenues of our bank."

The sound of that caused Jabari's antennas to rise. "What do you mean?"

Shrugging her shoulders, Sarah smirked. "Whatever you want it to mean. You're a handsome young man. I think that I can show you the ropes to getting your credit right and maneuvering through here for a great stay with our facility."

Placing the number in his pocket, Jabari looked her up and down. "Hopefully, you do personal classes. I'm not good with learning while a lot of people are around."

"I'm sure I can make that happen for you. That number is always available for use." Sarah smiled before pointing to the next customer behind him.

"Oh, my bad. Go ahead sir." He allowed the man to step in front of him.

"Thank you, Sarah." He waved lightly before heading towards the exit. All she could do was laugh and return his gesture. Getting outside, Jabari quickly pulled out his throwaway cellphone and entered the group chat Leo created for their crew last night. Typing in the words After School, he sent it and placed it back into his pocket. Within ten minutes of being in the bank, he spotted all the things he needed to know.

It was only one wack ass security guard monitoring the spot. He carried a strap no bigger than a nine-millimeter handgun. The building had over six cameras. Four on the inside and two on the outside. The bank only carried four drawers in the front where the tellers stood. Three females and one man. The job was sweet as pie. If they were just going for the money behind the counter, the job wouldn't take no more than one minute. All they needed was to get in and get out. Turning around to scope the bank out one last time, he thought about the girl Sarah. Her number was definitely about to come in handy. Jabari's palm was itching and the feeling was like no other. It was time to make their move soon.

Chapter 5

After tearing down Arden Fair Mall for over two hours, Jabari splurged out and bought all he could for Brandon's spoiled ass. It was hard not to spend it all when his little brother was used to not having shit when it came down to expense of his older brother. He knew that a price didn't matter. Jabari would come off his own shit in order to see the young one smile, and that's what it was about today.

In two hours, he had purchased four pairs of new Jordan's sneakers, seven different Nike and Puma outfits, plus new socks and different graphic T's that would excite him for sure. It was only simple things for himself. A black pea coat, black jeans and, of course, a black pair of Louis Vuitton high boots with the black scarf to match. Clothes didn't really matter when it came down to Jabari's swag. He knew for a fact that an image was definitely held inside and not on the clothes you wore.

There wasn't a day that went by where he stressed the issue about not having anything because shit like that just didn't mean anything to him. It was different for Brandon, especially when you were in the eighth grade and all the kids were wrapped up in the hype on who had the newest iPhone or the newest pair of kicks. It was common to compete and if you weren't up to par with your shit, you got talked about and picked on.

That was one rule he always tried to teach his younger brother. Never accept the same goals and path as another man because they were always bound to lead you astray. Being your own man meant more than just standing up. It meant to have your own brain when it came down to moving in the world. Most niggas thrived off worrying about some shit that didn't even involve them like where you stayed or how you dressed. That was always Jabari's reason for moving so discreet and not entertaining everybody as a friend.

After rounding up all the bags of shit he purchased for Brandon, he knew that complaining shouldn't even be placed in his category anymore. He had more than enough to finish out the last three months of middle school. There was more if he could maintain his grades and focus on the shit he needed in order to pass on to high school.

It had been a while since Jabari was able to move around, so when he spotted the opportunity to get some free space and air, he used it wisely. Of course, skipping school wasn't a usual habit for the straight A student, but lately his future was seeming to be directed towards the life of a refugee.

He didn't need the government jobs and the welfare care that most of the people tried their best to snatch from the DFCS assistant centers. Having money for the man in charge wasn't a blessing. It was a cult of motherfuckers cuffing to make it seem like they were just so successful when in reality they were just passing it down through their generations. That was the reason Jabari wanted his money in full, twenty acres and a mule. Whatever the folks owed him, he wanted it and damn sure wasn't gonna stop until he got it.

Listening to the J. Cole album on his cellphone, he played the song "Window Pain". The strong words from the rapper on the single always forced him to think harder. What else could he do better or what would it take to survive and be great within the world? It always added up to the same shit. Get money and make yourself relevant. Strolling down the side street of the mall, he spotted the small bakery and decided to grab his weekly dose of cheesecake. Out of all things he cherished, there was nothing like sitting alone to enjoy an original cheesecake from a local spot in his city. The taste was like none other. It was one of the only things he was willing to spend his paper on daily, if necessary.

As he walked in front of the large glass window, he spotted the beautiful Italian girl who was always behind the counter. It seemed like she never went home or she was either the only employee. Within three years of coming to the same bakery, he never witnessed a day that she wasn't present in the establishment flashing that big ole smile to everyone. Jabari entered the spot and placed all of his bags at a table before heading towards the counter. Before he could speak, the beautiful woman at the register smiled. "Hey," her voice was so angelic, and sweet.

Jabari couldn't help but to blush. Her sexy olive skin was butter smooth. Her slanted grey eyes gave her the look of a super model. Long black hair laid gently down her back, nearly to the top of her butt. Her hips and body was magnificent to be on a chick who wasn't over 5'6" and nothing from his hood could ever touch a woman like that, especially if she had an Italian dad who was ready to slice a nigga in two like a bagel about his princess.

"Hey. Can I have an original personal cheesecake please?" he asked politely. It was crazy because Jabari had never felt nervous around any woman. Every time he made an appearance in the eatery, his stomach would turn to butterflies when he spotted her. Still after years of coming in the place, he had yet to hold one conversation with the beauty.

"One cheesecake and one small iced tea, right?"

Looking in her eyes, he nodded. "Yes, one iced tea. How did you know that's what I wanted?"

"Because you've been ordering the same thing for two years. I've always seen you come in here and nothing has changed." She grabbed the money from his hand and gave him a receipt. "I'll bring your order over when its ready."

"Thank you," he said with a hint of nervousness. Instead of continuing to watch her mesmerizing eyes break into his soul, he walked off and took a seat at the small round table.

It was always hard when he thought about how he wanted his life to be with a woman. Jabari truly didn't favor or care for most of the girls he by passed during his life in California. There was no such thing as a first love, a girl he wanted to marry at first sight, or a chick that he was willing to risk getting in the bed with. That was until he spotted the lovely Italian Queen who he didn't have enough courage to approach. After years of seeing her face, he still couldn't find the best words to say in order to get to know her better. It was a down shot with the mean boss lady who always mugged behind the counter. She was the main baker, which was probably her mama. They resembled each other heavily, but her approval would definitely be needed when it came down to a girl of her race and quality.

After twenty minutes of waiting patiently, the mystery girl slid over to his table with a cheesecake balanced in her palm and his iced tea in another. "Here you are. One cheesecake and one iced tea. Can I get you anything else?" she asked politely.

"Yes. You could sit down and have a slice with me if it's not too much to ask," Jabari said while looking down at his cake. He didn't know how the hell that spilled out, but he was damn sho glad that he finally said something. That shit was like a fresh breath of air.

"Umm. Sure. I don't think I'm that busy where I could deny a piece of my mother's cheesecake," she said before taking a seat across from him.

Using his fork to cut her a piece, he placed it on a napkin and slid it over to her. "You can have some of my tea if you want," he said like a little kid offering something to his best friend. She could tell he was nervous and it was obviously the first time where he was able to have a one on one with a woman.

"No thank you. If you don't mind me asking, what is your name?"

"Uhhh Jabari. My name is Jabari and I'm eighteen." He nodded before biting a piece of cheesecake.

She couldn't help but to giggle from his response. His hands were slightly shaking and his eyes couldn't look at her without down casting every few seconds.

"Are you okay?" She brushed her long hair to the side and crossed her leg.

"Of course. What makes you ask that?" Jabari said biting another piece of his dessert.

"Because you won't look at me."

Fumbling with his fork, he stuttered before clearing his throat, "I mean-you know, uh, you're very beautiful, and-like I was gonna talk, but your mom makes me nervous. She hasn't taken her eyes off me since you've came over here," he said, cutting his eyes over to the Italian woman standing behind the register.

Laughing, she patted his hand. "That's just the way she is. She's the one who encouraged me to come and talk to you. Trust me. That look is for me, not you. It's more of her good luck face. She doesn't smile often, but her heart is more golden than a twenty-four-karat brick."

"But what do you need luck for? You're beautiful," Jabari complimented her before biting into his cheesecake again. The way her eyelids fluttered caused his heart to pace faster. Her rosy red cheeks, complimented her perfect thirty-two teeth smile. Her eyebrows were on point and whatever perfume she wore was knocking his love senses into submission.

"Thank you," she snickered.

"I never got your name?" Jabari was a little more relaxed to look up at her.

"Victoria."

Jabari could feel the shift of his heartbeat just from her name. She was surely something spectacular to even call a friend. It was shocking that she was sitting in front of him, when he randomly pondered about her long before she even had a name in his head.

"I like it. Is this just you and your mom's bakery?"

"Yeah. It was left from my grandad. My mom is more of our Italian cooking side of the family. She isn't happy without a stove and something sweet to bake." Victoria watched her mother pull out a fresh box of cake mix.

"How old are you?"

Victoria intertwined her fingers with a smirk. "I'm twenty-one."

"No way. You look like you're sixteen. I've been watching you for two years and there ain't no way you were nineteen back then."

"Mama, how old am I?" Victoria yelled out.

"Twenty one, and a pain in my ass for all twenty-one years. Is this young handsome man finally here to marry this stiff piece of daughter I have? I surely need her off my hands." She winked but continued moving around the bakery like a true professional.

Jabari couldn't help but to laugh. It was rare where you saw a mama pushing the daughter to date. Definitely when you were Italian and it was a black kid out of Sacramento. Staring at Victoria with excitement, he chuckled. "It's serious if your mom wants you to talk to a guy. I would have thought it was maybe the other way around."

"I'm different. I'm more of a school and house bug. Never really been interested into the whole relationship thing with every guy I see. I just happened to say something to mom about you when you walked in front of the bakery. I asked if she was familiar with you coming in and buying a cheesecake with the small iced tea." Victoria laughed.

"Really? I'm glad that you can remember small things like that about me because I'm a hard person to learn as well. I gotta tighten up when I'm around you," he replied with a playful tone.

"It's no need. I can already see what type of man you are. I see that you're different." She crossed her legs and sat back with a confident expression.

"Please tell me?" Jabari raised an eyebrow upon hearing her statement.

"Well, I can tell that you're educated because your speech is impeccable. I see that you have a strong passion within you as well. Not sure if it's more of a poetic passion or a Black determination passion, but it's one of them. You like to be a leader. It's always in your posture when you walk in. Your attitude shows me that you're a loner, but you also have a great sweet side to you. One that you're not comfortable with showing often." Victoria gazed at him knowing she hit the nail on point with his dark demeanor.

Nodding with a smile, Jabari lightly clapped. "That's better than anyone has ever gotten in my whole life. Even my dad. I guess I came in and bought too much cheesecake from your mom's shop."

"It doesn't take that many times to figure someone out. You are an image of how you move in this world is what my father use to tell me. First impression is always the main reason for a lot of people's failure with things throughout life. Move to impress and ignore the rest. I like the way you carry yourself. Quietly. Just how my family lives," she boosted his ego.

"Thank you. I mean this is kinda hard being that I've never got a chance to really meet you, but I will take whiff at it. I know that your favorite color is white. You go to college at Sacramento State judging from the T-Shirts I've seen you were occasionally. Your mom feels like you're not interested in men because you stay in the nest a lot. It's more of you not wanting to allow trust in your section because things have crumbled in your world before. I know that you use light make up. Maybe a little eyeliner and light black lipstick. You're also interested in me, but don't know how to tell me."

Victoria's words were caught in her throat from his theory and he was past correct. A man had never spoken on her favorite color and no one was ever able to know that she was closer to her mother than anyone in the world. Italians catered to family and after her father was murdered when she was younger, her mom was all she had left to hold on to. Jabari proved that he was obviously watching more than she expected.

"How did you know all of that just by watching me? Are you a spy?" She giggled and leaned closer to him.

"Nah, no spy. First impression, remember? Move to impress and forget the rest," he quoted her father's saying before rising to his feet.

"Are you leaving?" She looked as if her entire world would crash down if he was to say yes. The company of a man was rare in her life and he was definitely showing that could possibly be changed from the strong interest he kept contained inside of him.

Jabari looked at his watch. It was eleven-thirty, and he needed a few hours to prepare the move he had set up with Keyno the day before. "Unfortunately, I have to go. However, I would love to meet back with you soon, if it's possible."

"Is that a date?" Victoria grinned.

"Only if you allow it to be, and dress to impress." He smiled before holding out his hand for her to shake.

Embracing his gesture, she exhaled lightly when he kissed her hand delicately. His lips were like warm air grazing her skin on a summer morning. His dark eyes looked up into hers before he left. "Thank you for making me smile today. Is there a way that I can reach you? I would love to come and share some more cheesecake with you whenever we have the extra time," Jabari offered.

Victoria grabbed a paper napkin and used the pen from her work apron to scribble down her digits. "Hopefully, I can see you keep your word on that." She handed him the paper and stood up to return back behind the counter with her mother.

Jabari watched her for a few more seconds and could feel the love train disperse as she headed back for work. Her long beautiful hair was wisping as the light air blew from the A.C. unit inside the bakery. Victoria turned around and locked eyes with him. All he could do was wave before departing from the shop.

Stepping out of the bakery with a new smile, Jabari looked at Victoria's number before placing it into his pocket. That was a journey he definitely wanted to endure with the Italian princess. Her aura was beyond loveable. She had the spirit of a wife without a doubt, but at that time, money was calling Jabari's name like a siren to put out a fire. The tables surely wasn't gonna put food on itself and thinking about how happy Brandon would be gave him the feeling that he truly handled that business for the young one.

Pulling out his cell, he called Keyno's phone number. It rang three times before he picked up. "Yoo who this?"

"It's me, big bro."

"Bari? Where are you? You need to come get with me while I'm in the hood. I got that info for you," he confirmed.

"Cool. I'll be there in about twenty minutes. Where are you?"

"I'm at the corner store. Me and Blow. I'll be sitting down here waiting but not for long." Keyno hung up the call.

Sliding the phone back into his pocket. He picked up the bags and took flight. It was finally time to break Keyno in with the big plans. Robbing houses was for low budget niggas and after Jabari proved himself with this move, it would be the moment he showed them all how to take some true paper. The legit way.

Chapter 6

It was around 12:24 when Jabari got back to the house, placing the purchased shoes and clothes into Brandon's closet After being sure that he didn't touch anything to alert Ronald of him skipping school, he locked back up the crib and headed down the street to the nearest corner store. That walk didn't take longer than ten minutes, and he could see Keyno's big ass Cadillac Escalade from down the street. The speakers was so loud in his trunk that Jabari could literally feel the ground shake under his feet as he got closer. Blow was caked up in the passenger seat with the young girl from the hood known as Heather. Her check was fat. Her ass was fat, and all she liked to speak about was fat bankrolls coming to her pocket. The only nigga she seemed to show any love for was Blow.

Keyno, on the other hand, was having his way with a fine honey named Strawberry. Her red skin was flawless. Tattoos covered her bright skin and her body was gorgeous from head to toe. She didn't have to cake her face up with makeup like the rest and she was a grown piece of coochie in the hood who was used to being laced with the money and the finest jewels. Every drug dealer in the neighborhood wanted to cuff the beauty, but she was picky with the way she played in the streets. Only a few of the niggas in the hood could say they ever had a chance to even taste Strawberry. Her ass was that fine. She was the real meaning of that ass being big like the sun. Her clothes were always designer. Plus, her nails, and hair was constantly on fleek. That was without the help of a man. Strawberry was even in the loop with selling weight. She was one of the head bitches in charge down in

Hagginwood for real. Keyno had her wrapped up in a tight hug as if she was prepared to slip away at any second. Her hot red hair was laid gently down to her shoulders and the black tights on her body showed all the goodies she had to offer.

"Wassup, Keyno? You ready to talk, big bro?" Jabari stopped a short distance from him and spoke. He didn't want to push all up on him, especially when he was caked up with one of the baddest out the hood.

"Wassup, lil nigga?" He waved him over before kissing Strawberry on her lips. "Baby, this is my young one I was telling you about. He gonna pop like his big bro once he sprout out them million-dollar ideas. He's a fucking genius."

"Hey, Jabari. I've heard a lot about you with ya lil cute ass. Don't be running behind Keyno and forget about those million-dollar plans cause his ass couldn't care less about money." She popped the back of Keyno's head lightly.

Jabari smirked before Strawberry pinched his cheek and walked off towards her car. "Bye, boy. If you don't answer later on like you promise, I'm cutting yo ass off forever. Heather bring yo ass on before Blow have to drop you off tonight," she shouted towards her friend, who still occupied the front seat of Keyno's truck with her man.

It did take long for Heather to think about what Strawberry said before she jumped out of Blow's lap with the quickness. "I'll see you tomorrow. I'm gone, big head."

"I gotta big head for you. Just wait 'til tomorrow." He grabbed on his crotch with anticipation of sliding in between all that booty she had on her back. Her young ass was in for a tasty treat of the nasty games and Blow was gonna be sure to punish her just from the little trickery she liked to play.

"So wassup, my young one? You think y'all gonna be ready tonight?" Keyno asked Jabari before firing up a blunt. Blow hopped out of the truck and made his way over into their conversation.

Jabari ain't have shit to hide, so he didn't mind speaking in front of Blow's lame ass. "We will be ready. This is kinda simple, Keyno. I wanna fast forward the small kiddie meals and really bring something to the table with you."

"What's that?"

Jabari listened to the music quake and moved over towards the driver seat to turn that shit down.

"What the hell you doing, lil nigga? That shit was up for a reason, nigga!" Blow said while he broke down a cigarillo.

"Not when we talking about business, nigga. That shit too loud," Jabari addressed before turning back around to Keyno. "Like I said big bro, I got bigger moves for us. I've been doing my research. I got the bank down on Arden Way and I know we can handle them with four men. It's one security guard, four bank tellers. It's an easy move if we got the right timing with going in. I even been keeping an eye out on the bank truck that's been making the drops," Jabari lied just to make the shit sound official. He was so ready to take back what was his that it was itching just speaking about the matter.

"Wait. When did you find out all of this?" Keyno pulled on the blunt Blow passed him.

"Today, I went an opened a bank account and scoped out all the shit that we needed to know. Within a week, we should be able to go in that bitch and be out within seconds. Easy cake. The front drawers only hold up to seventy thousand dollars, which is like eighteen in each drawer. With Me, Teddy, and Leo that shit will be a piece of pie. I'll break you off for using the guns, and just to show you how sweet it is, I'ma record if for you," he replied with confidence.

"Oh, you dat sure, huh?" Keyno passed the blunt to Jabari. Blow was looking all sentimental and shit like the young one was trying take his place, but what he didn't know was Jabari truly held the heart to be a leader. His mind wasn't letting shit pass him without being aware of what damage it could cause and no one could infiltrate against them when there was no such things as getting down with the crew.

"I'm sure, Keyno. You know I don't like when you second guess me. This is it."

"You keep saying that you ready for a bank, but we ain't seen you even tackle something simple like a house lick, young one. That's like you telling me you can make a platinum album and haven't put out one mixtape." Blow waved him off with disbelief.

"You don't know what I can do because I've never did it alone, Blow. I can do it before you and get away without causing a scene like you. I'm smarter." Jabari looked at him arrogantly.

"Hey calm down. No beefing when the business in the air." Keyno popped his trunk looking at both of them with a stern look. "Come here Jabari," he said as he raised the trunk door up higher.

The pistols and assault rifles that he laid his eyes on was like a toy soldier store. AK's Carbon 15s Glocks, Rutgers, and even silencers to ensure that the missions is handled quietly.

Keyno picked up a chrome 45 automatic and handed it to Jabari. "This is yours. It's my favorite gun, but it's yours now, so don't play if you gon' use it. These other babies is for the crew, but just in case shit get ugly, I'm sending Blow in there with y'all. I can't risk none of you getting hurt. Blow will kill of necessary, lil bro."

Jabari exhaled before looking over at his hating ass. He was just like a dick rider, smiling when Keyno spoke as if he was the second in charge. Instead of entertaining him, he placed his attention back on what was at hand. "Cool. But I'm letting a nigga know right now, I'm in charge when we step in there. I don't want nobody getting hurt and this nigga is a renegade."

"Sounds like a scary nigga to me," Blow teased.

"Not scary, it's being smart. I'm not about to go to jail for a murder about petty coins when I can get a five to ten-year bid for sweeping out an entire bank safe. Like I said, I'm in charge."

"I agree," Keyno said with a smile.

"What!" Blow stressed with anger in his tone.

"You heard me. The young one is in charge. You can't expect him to show his skills if he can't take the lead. If a nigga moves wrong, handle your business. But if not, let him run that shit." Keyno placed a clip into one of the choppas and racked the chamber back. "Remember, this isn't about our feelings. I love both of y'all to death, but if y'all think this is a competition, then both of y'all have lost already. Stop that negativity between each other."

Blow shrugged with a smile. "I'm good. The one thing I know is that I kill shit for fun. Don't make it my fault if one of y'all niggas get slumped playing the fucking role."

"And if anything happens to them, I'll deal with you. Just because you feel like you can protect yourself doesn't mean that you aren't supposed to guard them as your little brothers. Y'all all going in together and y'all coming out that bitch as one. Period. If you feeling another way besides the one I just explained, speak your peace now." Keyno folded his arms and looked at both of them.

Sensing that Blow wasn't gonna oblige first, Jabari held out his hand and shook Keyno's. He knew that big bro was the truth, and trust meant everything when it came down to running with him. He never led him wrong before, so if Blow was a part of the mission, then so be it. No matter how he looked at it. No one was going to go against the rules he had set. The mission was to start taking banks. If it took one correct robbery to prove himself to Keyno, then it was done. "I'm with it," Jabari said with respect.

"I'm with it too," Blow said as if he wouldn't let the young one beat him at shit.

"Good. Now that y'all on the same page, I can give y'all a run down. It's three niggas in the spot. Forty thousand in cash. The rest is free for all which means if you find it, you keep it. Now, don't get this confused. This is for both of y'all. No one should cuff on the cheddar. Period. All cash is a direct split. I'm only saying this because I know you, Jabari, but that don't mean your clique will be on the same page. I'm not tolerating disloyalty," Keyno warned.

"I got them, Keyno. Period. They gonna listen to me anyway," Jabari assured.

"Cool. Now like I said, Blow is my shooter, so if he feels that a nigga gotta be handled, you move with him. The worst thing during a robbery is to show dysfunctions between the niggas who laying the shit down. I need y'all to focus, make it quick, and get this bread. If this goes accordingly, we can see what y'all wanna do with the bank next."

"Bet," Jabari said before giving Keyno a pound. Tapping Blow up, he looked him I'm the eyes. "Tonight, we will be ready. Just leave the bad energy at home and let's go and get this money."

"I was about the say the same shit, young one. I salute you. Let's eat." Blow nodded before watching him walk off.

Keyno looked over to Blow with a smile.

"What?" he asked, wondering what the smirk was for.

"You know what, nigga. That boy solid. He deserves a chance."

Blow grinned. "Just like you told me when I first started. It's nothing personal, but you gotta make the cut in order to be on the team. Let the nigga earn that shit like I did," Blow said before walking off to get inside the truck.

Keyno smirked as he watched Jabari walk back down inside of the hood. He knew for a fact that his feelings were always on point. It was something special about Bari that he liked. His ambition was so similar to his own. He knew that Jabari was meant to be a real taker and he was positive that shit was gonna change the game for Hagginwood.

Chris Green

Chapter 7

After kicking it with the fellas for the next few hours, Jabari looked at his watch and knew that it was close to dinner time in his home. Ronald would definitely shit a brick if he wasn't present for that fake ass prayer over the food. The sun was going down gently, the night was young and full of life. The mission was set to go down at eleven o'clock tonight and by the time he knew that Ronald would be pass long gone in the bed. The lick shouldn't take his crew more than twenty minutes to move in and come back swiftly as if he was never gone. At midnight, he wanted to be sitting in his bed counting a bundle of bills to add with the shit he already stashed.

Making his way through the front door, Ronald and his brother was sitting at the table as if they had been waiting for hours. Without wasting time, Jabari moved over to the sink and washed his hands. Grabbing a paper napkin, he wiped them dry before taking his seat. Ronald was eyeing him with anger but bowed his head to say grace.

"Lord, I ask you to guide us. Keep this family sane and grateful for the small things. Your blessing for waking up is good enough. Give us more understanding with that," he said dryly before cutting his eyes at Jabari. "Amen."

The funny action caught Jabari off guard, but he expected him to probably be mad about coming in twenty minutes late. As he picked up his fork and began to fill his plate, he noticed Brandon sitting with a vexed expression in his face. "What's wrong with you, Champ?"

Shaking his head silently, he continued to eat his dinner.

Jabari happened to notice Ronald grilling him heavily. His foot was rocking heavily and he had yet to touch his plate. The nigga was usually busting that shit in seconds like he was still in the prison cafeteria, but tonight, he was obviously feeling salty about something.

"You a'ight?" Jabari looked at him curiously.

"I should be asking you the same thing?" he fired back quickly.

Sitting down his fork, he leaned back in his seat. "Look, I'm sorry about walking in here twenty minutes late, Pop, but that ain't no reason to grill me down like you wanna fight," Jabari addressed.

"Fuck coming in here twenty minutes late. I wanna know where the hell you spending yo time, nigga?" Ronald spat loudly.

"What are you talking about and why are you yelling? That's only gonna make me angry." He brushed off his attitude, knowing his temper could rise hastily.

"Nigga, I don't give a fuck about you getting angry in my house little boy. Where the fuck did you get all these damn clothes?" Ronald said picking the shopping bags up from the floor to sit them on the table.

Brandon rolled his head in disappointment. "Man, I don't got no clothes, dad," he whined.

"Shut the hell up before I slap you, boy," he barked with a nasty tone.

Jabari stood up with a heated frown. "Yo chill the fuck out, Pop. Don't talk to him like that." His aura said that he definitely wasn't fucking playing.

"You don't tell me how to talk to my son, neither do you tell me what the fuck to say in my damn house. I found this shit in Brandon's closet, Jabari. Where did it come from?"

He said, pulling the expensive gear out the bags.

"I bought it for him."

"Yeah. Where in the fuck did you get the money? You ain't paid no bills around this bitch and I damn sho' and seen you walk in with a job yet. How did you afford all this?" Ronald mugged him demanding his damn answer.

"A friend."

"A friend." Ronald chuckled before slanging all the clothes on the floor and stood to his feet. "Nigga, I don't know if you think that I got shitted out the coochie yesterday or if you been smoking crack before you walked back into my home, don't no friends give out handouts that's worth about two-thousand dollars," he said holding to the receipt.

Jabari folded his arms and sat down. "I made some extra money and bought my brother some clothes. What's the big deal? It didn't come out of your pockets."

Ronald balled go his fist angrily. "That's the problem, boy. If it ain't come out of my pocket, that means it was taken out of somebody else's. I don't like dirty cash in my spot, especially if you out there doing some dumb shit that could put my home in jeopardy. I know you hanging with that older cat, Keyno. So, what you doing, dealing dope or robbing?"

"Maybe both," Jabari stated arrogantly.

"And if you are, you're gonna pack your shit and get the fuck out of my home. I'm not allowing it the illegal way in here, playa. I did fifteen long years for the same shit and I refuse to see any of it around me or my family again, Jabari." He was now standing firm in case he had try and remove his son by force.

Jabari rubbed his temples and looked up at his father. "You work a job making seven dollars an hour and you expect to think we about to survive. I love ya, Pop, but being like you isn't on my agenda. I'm striving to have my own everything and I refuse to see my brother suffer when you know that taking care of him is a hardship on you. We barely have meals to last us until the weekend. You live check to check, Ronald. How is this family being fed?" he questioned aggressively.

"Maybe it isn't much, but I'm trying, Jabari. The world ain't perfect, son. What if you die behind the hands of taking someone's property? What if your family dies? My old life is what I left alone in order to see you, and your brothers face every day I wake up," Ronald said, nearly on the verge of tears. "I love you, son, but if you not returning this stuff, and letting go of those friends of yours tonight, I won't allow you to rest your ass under my roof. So, what's it's gonna be? Because I'm not up to debating with a teenager."

Jabari looked at his little brother's sad face and could tell that he was about to beg him not to leave. Unfortunately, being a puppet for his dad's enslaved mind state was not about to occur. The polluted senses of the Black people today were obey and receive a small pay. When in reality, the check was already overdue. The people was just killing them softly like Lauryn Hill. It grabbed their mind through the televisions and social media to be a puppet, to gravitate or be left behind. That was a risk that Jabari would just have to take. Before he laid down and just died as a black man, he was gonna rise up and be the Black guy who the man couldn't touch.

"I'm leaving. I'll be gone in fifteen minutes," he said before walking off to his room.

Stepping through the small eight by nine room, Jabari grabbed his large suitcase from the closet and began to throw his small amount of clothes inside. He knew that it was surely no walking back after this. Being out on his own only meant that his actions were for a purpose. It was officially time to grow up and show his cotton pickin dad what the real meaning of a man was. He knew that Brandon was surely not about to be deprived by his own race and wallow in sorrow for being raised up without a purpose. He wanted the young champ to know that his brother was different. The refugee who was against any oppression and made a way though the hands of all the people who was assisting the crooked ass White House. Rich was gonna be an understatement. Wealthy was were his mind attached on too, and it wasn't changing. Period.

Grabbing his black history books, he pulled the grey bag full of cash from underneath the old floorboard in his closet and walked back over to his suitcase. Tossing the bag around his back, he grabbed the large travel bag and spotted Brandon coming through the bedroom door. His eyes were welling up and he could see that he wasn't digging the idea of his older brother leaving him stranded.

"Man, Jabari. Just take me with you. Please?" He grabbed his shirt in a pleading manner.

He could feel Brandon's nervousness and didn't want to leave him uneasy. Lifting up his head with a finger, Jabari mugged him. "What's wrong? You know I'm not gonna leave you here for long. It's only for right now."

The look on Brandon's face couldn't hold the tears. Shaking his head repeatedly, he cried out in agony. "Just don't leave me here, man. Jabari, I really wanna come with you. I'm not safe here." He looked back to see if their dad was in the area to eavesdrop.

Jabari looked at him with a look of anger. "What do you mean you're not safe? From who, Ronald?"

"Yes. I just don't want you to leave, man." He cut the idea of speaking the truth to his older brother.

"Brandon, has he ever put his hands on you?"

His look told it all, but he still chose to lie. "Nah."

Jabari sensed that he wasn't being honest but tucked it into his back pocket. "Look, give me two months and I'm gonna come back to get you. I'm gonna get this bread right, get my own place, and make sure you can eat the way you want. I just need you to trust me." He glared into Brandon's eyes with sincerity.

"Please," he begged. "Just don't forget about me, Jabari."

"You're my brother, champ. I can't forget you. You're all I got and I'ma take care of you by any means." He reached into his pocket and peeled his little young one five-hundred dollars. Forcing it into his pocket. He tapped the side of his head. "Don't tell him about that. Stay quiet and wait for me. Go to school and don't stress. Trust me," Jabari assured.

Wrapping his older brother in a hug, he walked back out of the room directly beside him. Jabari looked up at Ronald with no respect in his posture before speaking, "If anything happens to him, I'm not doing any talking. Period," he threatened indirectly before leaving out the front door.

Walking across the lawn, he called Keyno's phone. Just when he thought that he wouldn't receive an answer, he picked up on the fifth ring. "Wassup, young one?

"I just got kicked out, Keyno. I need you to come and get me."

"Kicked out? That nigga, Ronald, playing like that?" he said with a distasteful voice.

"I'm walking through the hood right now. I got all my clothes on me. Are you coming to get me or do I need to take a car?" Jabari cut all the small talk.

"Meet me down at the block, the store parking lot. I'll be there in about fifteen minutes. Don't go nowhere, man. I'm on the way," Keyno said before hanging up.

Placing the cell back in his pocket, he headed for the block. A man was what his dad wanted, and that's exactly what he was about to get.

***

4 hours later
Village 5

The outside of the neighborhood felt like a nigga was waiting for death. The projects were surrounded by niggas with no goals and people who were trying to swivel anything a motherfucker had to offer. In the mix of the chaotic black sectioned space of Sacramento, a true money maker by the name of Beep was pushing dope out a trap like it was legit. The man's spot was bumping like he owned a fucking candy shop on Kiddie Avenue.

Leo, Teddy and Steven sat quietly waiting for Jabari to give the okay. Being that Steven was already an expert driver, his position in every lick was already placed. He could get away from a gang of cheetahs with a gazelle strapped around his back if he had to. He wasn't a gangsta by a long shot but escaping away from cops was like a *Grand Theft Auto* game to him.

Teddy and Leo, on the other hand, were always hungry and eager. That's what gave them the most perfect team.

The only oddball was Blow, who mumbled some smart shit every thirty seconds in the back seat.

Jabari ignored him and continued to stare at the house.

"Why in the fuck are we waiting? Them niggas in there?"

Blow asked impatiently.

"I'm waiting for Keyno's call. He told me not to move until I got the call, so just chill the fuck out," he spat, hating the idea of him coming on any move with his crew.

"A call? Nigga, Keyno probably fucking a bitch and you telling me we waiting on a call," Blow stressed.

"Yeah, nigga. That's what I just said." Jabari began to grow angry.

"Watch yo mouth, young one. Remember I'm not ya bitch ass daddy," Blow spat.

Before Jabari could turn around and reply, his cell rang loudly giving him the cue. Without hesitation he pulled his chrome 45 from the hip and jumped out. Blow, Leo, and Teddy was directly behind him. The stupid argument was surely about to go viral, so the angels were definitely watching over them to get the smooth lick over, and quickly.

Moving swiftly up to the door. Jabari wasted no time kicking in the door with a hard, right foot. His force was so strong that bitch came off the hinges. Leo, Teddy, and Blow didn't waste any time speeding in behind him. The dudes who occupied the living room tried to scatter and failed horribly.

Leo slapped the first dude he could into the chokehold. Jabari knocked the nigga who looked like the leader clean over his glass table with a slap to the head.

"Broooo what the fuckkk? Who are you, fool, and what the fuck did I do to you, man?" he folded quicker than expected.

Jabari stuffed the pistol in his mouth and placed a finger up to his own lips. "Be quiet, relax and don't die. It'll be over very quickly."

Blow contained the other male who tried to escape for the bedroom. A hard slap from the AK. 47's handle, he crumbled to sleep like a junkie passing out with a balled-up dollar in their hand.

Two females sat with their hands up on the couch, but neither one of them uttered a single word. One was Black, and the other was White. Teddy moved over to them with a distraught face. "Y'all hoes ever been in the ghetto before?"

"No, we just moved down the street. We go to college in San Diego," the Black saddity chick stuttered quicker than porky the pig.

"Well guess what? Welcome. This is a robbery and I need both of y'all fine asses to hit the floor. Asses up. Face down," he growled with a fake menacing tone.

The girls did what they were told. Face down, ass up with no sign of disagreeing with them at all.

"That's right. Make sure ya tongue on the floor," he continued to rant.

Jabari cleared his throat and looked at him stupidly. "Please just stop." Placing his attention back on the coward in front of him, he removed the gun from his mouth. "Okay, buddy. We're here to take the cash. I need it. If you lie, I'll kill all of you. You got five seconds," Jabari said before looking at his watch.

The nigga began to panic before one second could even pass. "Kill? Nigga, I ain't said I was bucking, but I'm warning you. This ain't my shit. The money is in the kitchen under the table," he spilled the beans with his chest pumping profusely in fear of being shot.

"Ted, check it. Tear the whole thing up. Matter fact," Jabari pointed to the kitchen.

Teddy wasted no time and checked under the glass kitchen table. Sliding the brown checkerboard duffle from underneath, he opened it up and spotted the crispy blue Benjamins poking out.

"He damn sho wasn't lying. We got paper, guys." He dragged the bag over to Jabari and opened it.

Examining it closely, Jabari nodded and zipped it back up until Teddy finished his mission with the kitchen. After flipping cabinets, boxes, and can goods, he stumbled across three kilos of cocaine and seven pounds of marijuana.

"These niggas is the real cookie shop, y'all. They got it all." He walked back into the living room with the drugs in his hand.

"Fucking right. We splitting that," Blow said with his gun still on his sleep victim.

Jabari didn't respond to him. Instead, he looked back at the man who gave up all the so-called merchandise in his shit. "So, what's your name big guy?"

"Beep."

"Beep. That means you're the man in charge from what I've been hearing. Now, I'm not an expert Beep, but that's a lot of cash in that bag. You gave it up pretty quickly. Where the rest of it?"

"Man, fuck that shit! We got the drugs. We got the money. Let's go!" Blow yelled.

"Calm the fuck down and chill. I'm in charge of this shit. Remember?" He looked back at him before turning back around to the dork ass nigga Beep. "Answer the question."

He fidgeted and knew that he was not gonna be able to shake the hothead in his bumper, but he refused to lose it all.

"Young one, I gave you all of it. Spare me." He held his hands up like he did the most righteous deeds on earth.

"Spare you means leave the rest. So where is it?" Jabari placed the gun to his forehead.

"Bro, we've been here too long. I think it's really time to go." Leo looked around to be sure the street was still empty.

"Not yet. Where the fuck is it, Beep? Last chance."

Closing his scary ass eyes, he jerked his body like a bitch who lost her morning time dick. "The oven, man. It's inside the pizza boxes." He sweated bullets seeing the barrel down his face.

Teddy followed his directions and removed the pizza boxes from the oven. Opening them, his eyes landed on the crispy bills stacked inside. "Jackpot!" He grabbed them both and walked back into the living room. "We got it. Let's make it," Teddy confirmed.

The loud gunshot that rang out caught everybody off guard. Knowing that his mind wouldn't lead him wrong, Jabari looked back at Blow who stood over the man holding his neck. "Why the fuck did you shoot him?" He pushed Blow forcefully.

"Nigga, he bucked and reached for my gun." He shoved Jabari back.

"Hey, we can't do this love making shit right now. Let's just go," Teddy said with annoyance bumping through his body.

Jabari looked down at the bleeding man and knew he was nearly dead. The blood oozing from his wound was leaking heavily and he would surely drain out before a doctor could have a chance to arrive.

Jabari's lips shook with anger. Walking over to Teddy, he grabbed the three bricks out of his possession and walked towards the bathroom."

"Yo Bari, what are you doing?" Leo asked.

Stepping in the bathroom, he burst the packages and began flushing the product down the toilet. Cracking the last brick, he tossed it all over the floor and walked out. "Now, we can go."

"What the fuck did you just do with the work?" Blow asked with a crazy expression.

"I flushed it."

"Why the fuck did you do that?" he raged.

"Because we don't need it. Now let's go," Jabari ordered heading for the door.

Feeling the sharp rage shoot through his body, Blow raised his choppa and gunned down everybody who was occupying the home. He even walked over to the girls and placed a slug through their heads. The crew stood still and watched in horror. The entire time of them pulling home invasions and robberies, this was the first where they actually seen people lose their lives in the process.

Blow cracked his neck from side to side before brushing past Jabari and running out. The crew followed behind him not wanting to be caught on the scene of the terrible sight. Jabari's heart was in pain for the innocent lives being slain, but the only thing he could do was run once he heard the distant police sirens wailing through the air.

Chapter 8

Arriving back to Hagginwood, Steven pulled the throwaway car into Keyno's parking lot. Knowing that they were on the way back from the caper, he waited patiently outside until they arrived. Once the car was parked, Blow was the first one to jump out with his gun in hand. A mug was on his face as he moved towards Keyno giving the bad news without even opening up his mouth.

"What happened?" he asked with a straight face.

Jabari was the next to jump out with his vest off, wearing nothing but a tank top. He moved briskly towards Blow with his hands balled and Keyno knew what was coming next. Before he could swing, he jumped in the way. "Whoa, young one. What's the problem? What happened?" Keyno could read that his anger was obviously about something serious.

"Ask him." Jabari was ready to get with the action because talking was off his mind once they left those poor victims' crib.

Keyno glared at Blow. "So wassup?"

Blow laughed the young nigga off. "Man, a nigga reached for my pistol and I fired his ass up. This lil young nigga acted like I was at fault."

Keyno turned his face back to Jabari. "Lil bro, I told you how it worked."

"He didn't just shoot him, Keyno. He killed everyone in the fucking spot. This is why I didn't want to work with this clown!" he spat with his chest rising heavily.

"Yeah, I did nigga. That's after he flushed three fucking bricks of cocaine. This little nigga literally trashed seventy-five thousand dollars' worth of product. For what?" Blow yelled.

"Because it's crack, nigga. We rob. We don't sell dope, remember? You think I'm about to be the reason these black people destroying themselves because you wanna hold an image? Fuck you, nigga. We robbers for a reason. If you want more money, let's go get it. Anytime my hands touch or see any poison it's getting flushed. It slows the group down. Makes us get unfocused and it tear down the same community that I was raised in. My move, my rules, nigga."

Keyno grabbed Blow's gun and shook his head. "He's right."

"What! Keyno, you can't fucking be serious right now. This lil nigga is bugging and I don't deal with children when I make moves. I'm damn sho not interested in losing three bricks I could've sold for twenty-five grand a piece. How the fuck am I wrong, nigga?"

"Because. Just like he said. You're a robber, not a drug dealer. Nigga, I haven't touched a sack of dope in three years. I grabbed my easy paper and keep it pushing. We build the hood, nigga, not destroy it. If you wanna sell dope, get you a bomb and hit the block, baby boy. Right now, we takers and its bigger shit in place, so think about that shit and worry about how we finna spend this money." Keyno tapped Jabari on his shoulder to calm him down.

"I'm not working with him anymore if you ain't coming," Jabari said before walking back to the car.

Leo, Teddy, and Steven stood in the driveway with clueless faces. Leo stepped up first. "Look, I don't know about all this other shit, but let's count this cheese and come back to the rest of this shit later. I gotta make my way back home. It's too much going on."

"Exactly. Y'all niggas hit the back porch. I'll bring some beers and we will light up some bud. Let's count this shit and split down the prize. Fuck frowning," Keyno agreed before stepping through his front door.

It didn't take longer than forty-four minutes for Steven and Teddy to count up sixty-eight thousand dollars. Jabari sat on the far bench blowing a large Garcia Vega full of Kush. Blow walked around waiting for his cut, so he could peel off to Heather's spot for the rest if his night.

"We struck, so how much is that a piece?" Teddy looked at all them for an answer.

Steven used his powerful mind to estimate it quickly. "It's about eleven thousand and thirty-three dollars. There should be at least thirty-four cents left for all of us."

"No need, baby boy. Just hand me eleven and I'm out of here," Blow asked with his hand out.

Steven picked up the requested amount and placed it into his palm. Before he could turn to leave, Keyno called his name, "Blow?"

Turning around with a heated face, he smirked. "Yeah?"

"Remember that we're family, nigga. But we're still a team. You gotta learn more control and stop releasing that energy so hard, bro. You know what it's like to be a young one. Quit acting brand new."

"Man, I'm about to go get me some pussy, eat some Skittles and go to fucking sleep. Call me when it's time to work." Blow walked off shooting a bird in the air.

Steven broke the rest of the profits down evenly with the remaining men and stood to his feet. "I'm not trying to break away when the fun is heating up, but my mother will have a heart attack if she wakes up and I'm not there. I'm out." Steven threw the deuces and walked out of Keyno's back yard.

"Later, my guy." Jabari patted his back.

"Well, I guess I'ma slide out too because shit has been very hectic tonight. I'll scream at you dudes when the sun rises." Leo gave Jabari, Teddy, and Keyno a pound before pushing it behind Steven.

Jabari sipped on his beer and inhaled on the weed trying to release the thought of those innocent black lives that were spilled. Teddy shook his heads before raising the keys to their stolen car. "Uhhh, you know I need a ride home, so I guess I'll just take myself if it's not a problem."

"Nah, go ahead, my dude. Get some rest," Jabari said before embracing his brother with a hug.

Watching him leave and jump back inside the contaminated vehicle they committed the horrendous act in, he shook his head before looking over to Keyno. "I'm trying to shake the fact of killing my own people, big bro. It's not the way shit circulates in my mind. I'm against those crooked motherfuckers, not the man with color," he stated with a sad expression before toking on the weed in his hand.

Keyno downed the last of his Heineken and sparked his own joint. "I know you have a bright mind, young one. It's the reason I have so much faith in you. I know you have fight, courage, and principal in your veins. I love that shit, but you can't expect everybody to think like you, Jabari. You're meant to be a leader fighting for this motherfucking country. You have too much ambition and I'm afraid it's not gonna do no justice trying to speak it with the same people who rebel against that shit. I know you a real Malcolm X, Black Panther on the low. You ready to do it to the cops and all. That's you knowing your equal rights and breaking out of yo chains. Still to this day, young one, we have people that will never break free because the chains is all they know." Keyno shrugged hopelessly.

"And that doesn't anger you? I'll take from the White man's mouth before I keep torturing my people with the statistics that they've already built up against us, Keyno. It's stupid. No one respects the nigga who hurts the hood. We make it and come back to embrace the hood. Uplift it. I'm not comfortable with hurting people unless it's necessary," he said sternly.

Keyno couldn't disagree with the wise words from his young friend. The truth hurt worse than a bitch, definitely when he didn't have nothing to reply back with. "So, you rob knowing that people can get hurt. Does that make you just as guilty?"

"It does, but there's one difference Keyno."

"What's that?"

"My intentions. I'm not thinking of it, so more than likely my ride will be smooth and go accordingly if everybody fall in line. But a nigga sho looking for it will find a way to release that demon. It's a disease and it's born in all of us. Some people just can't learn what greater evil it does. When you disrespect the mercy, when you try to empower over everything as if you were Allah, you lose Keyno. I'm not trying to suffer harder than then burdens I've already placed upon my own soul. I can do it better." Jabari swigged on his Heineken.

Sitting down his bottle, Keyno looked him in the eyes. "So, you telling me that you can do it better. You can rob and do every move without murdering anyone? Because if you can, Jabari, you must be a spy working with Jason Statham from the *Transporter*?"

"Nah, I ain't him. I'm better, but I'm damn sure tired of being second guessed, Keyno." He smirked arrogantly.

"So if I give y'all whatever you need to handle this bank job, how long do you think it will take to get in, and out?" Keyno questioned with a hand on his chin.

"You really wanna know?" Jabari leaned forward with a smirk.

"Yeah. This is serious, so I do."

"Forty-five seconds."

"Bullshit." Keyno laughed off his response. He chuckled lightly until he noticed Jabari still holding a straight face. Leaning forward, he pulled the weed and passed it to him. "You're dead ass serious?"

"As a fucking heart attack." He pulled the good reefer and exhaled heavily.

Standing up, Keyno rubbed his hands together. "Well, let's take it inside and see what we come up with tomorrow."

Both of them entered the large home and Keyno locked the doors behind them after getting inside. Jabari looked around the magnificent vonsway home. It was decorated with a delicate touch of history and Black, strong Reggae vibes. The Jamaican pictures around the wall was flooded from the kitchen to the living room. The same history legends Jabari cherished were sitting around Keyno's home with every turn you could make. Madam CJ Walker. Harriet Tubman. Even his mentor Huey P. Newton. It was more of a museum in his eyes staring at all the priceless paintings. "Keyno, where did you get these?"

"I painted them, young one. That's my other talent I don't speak on. You know how it be. Just a lost dream I use to have."

"How is it a lost dream when you can remember something so special to our culture?"

Keyno stared around at his painted artwork and shrugged. "It's not able to be heard from every person, but what my paintings can't explain, there will be a good man like you willing to give the wisdom to fill in the blanks. I'm sure of it, young one," he responded before opening the guest room door. The large 60-inch flat screen television was the first thing Jabari spotted. A brand-new Xbox system was attached and the room decor was on point. The bed sheets and curtains where black with gold trimmings. Another legend for the black culture was hanging above the bed. "Who is that?"

Keyno chuckled thinking that the smart guy was just playing. After seeing that he was really waiting for an answer, he looked back at the painting. "That's George Washington Carver."

"Ohh, the man who whipped up the peanut butter," Jabari laughed. "I've read about him, but never seen his face."

"Yeah, that's him. Any piece of history you did for the black culture should be epic. They said we wouldn't never see a black President either, but I have one painted over my bed right now. It's like my second safe haven."

"What's the first?" Jabari asked wanting to see where his mind was.

"Robbing." He shrugged. "This is your room now. Clean up behind ya self. Wash the dishes behind ya self and do what the fuck you want to do," Keyno said before walking out of the room, closing the door behind him.

Jabari placed all his bags inside the closet and looked around at the sweet space of freedom. It felt like home, and it wasn't even his spot. That was surely coming soon with the mind frame he had stationed in his head. With the help of Keyno and his friends, Jabari was gonna snatch more money from the people than a scam artist had ever seen. It was only a matter of time.

Pouring out all the info about the bank on his bed, he scrolled through all the papers. Picking up the number, he pulled out his cell and dialed it quickly. After listening to it ring once, it was answered.

"Hello?" a woman answered in a groggy tone.

"Sarah?"

"Yes. Who is this?"

"You might not remember me, but my name is Jabari."

A small silence filled the line for a slight second before she spoke, "I remember you. The cute young guy from my job. I see that you're a late nighter."

Sitting down on the bed, he smiled. "I didn't mean to call so late, but I needed someone to talk to," he lied.

"Awww. Are you okay?"

"Yeah. I just really need advice," he admitted.

"Advice about what, sweetie?"

"About making you help me succeed. I need to know all about the bank you work in. Is that too much advice?" He closed his eyes hoping she wouldn't hang up.

"That depends, Jabari. Where do I fit into all of this?"

Smiling wickedly, he sat back and got comfortable. "Where would you like to fit in, Sarah? I'm willing to do whatever to make sure you're right next to me as I succeed."

Chapter 9

It was early the next morning when Jabari awoke from his sleep. Forgetting that he had school, he jumped upon as if the bus was gonna travel backwards in order to pick him up. It was nine fifteen and class had started almost twenty minutes ago. Looking at the money sprawled out on his floor, he picked it up and placed it into his grey duffle bag with the rest of his stash. Wiping the corners of his eyes, Jabari walked out into the living room. The flat screen mounted against the wall was stressing the death of Kobe Bryant and his daughter Gigi. Keyno was nowhere to be found and the common courtesy before creeping around somebody's shit was to make sure they knew you were awake and moving around.

Walking out on the front porch, He spotted Keyno in a deep conversation on his cellphone. Jabari flashed him the rolled-up joint he grabbed from off his bed, and he gave him the thumbs up. Knowing that it was nothing like that early morning high, he fired up the Cali Kush and passed it immediately. The horrible coughs he began to release clearly showed that he wasn't ready for the strong dosage. Keyno laughed and covered the phone. "Weak ass chest, nigga," he mumbled.

"Fuck you!" Jabari coughed violently with a middle finger in the air.

By the time he was done, Keyno was ending the call and broke out into a fit of laughter. "Young one, you good? Boy, I thought I was about to have to give CPR to yo ass out here while I was on the line. Let me find out you can't handle this gas," he teased, taking a giant puff of the chronic.

"I damn near thought I might need an ambulance for real." Jabari laughed while patting his chest lightly. "Who you was on the line with Ms. Strawberry?"

"Nah, I was hollering at a couple old relatives. They was speaking about my mama, so you know I had to soak as much of that in as possible. I never really got to be around her besides a little of my childhood. After the age of eight, it all seemed like a big dream. I can't even tell you her age." Keyno shook his head in disappointment.

"What happened to her if you don't mind me asking?" Jabari felt a slightly ache in his heart for his friend's history.

"She was on crack. That's about all I know. I can't really remember shit. My dad had me most of the time, but he was killed like fifteen years ago. Gunned down like a damn dog, man. That shit left me with nothing and nobody because my mom vanished right after. I never seen her again after that. I really don't even remember how the lady look. It's crazy, but it is what it is." He nodded accepting the fact of reality.

"My mom was on crack real bad also. She never shook back for me and my little brother either. She nearly went to mental health. Ronald did fifteen years and we were staying with a family friend the entire time. That's crazy our situation is similar. I always had the chance to go and visit my mama in the institution, but I just can't stand to see her act like that. It really pulled me away," Jabari said before accepting his blunt back.

"Listen young one, I wouldn't give a damn what position she's in. You go and spend as much time possible. It's no telling when she will leave this place. You only get one. Squash any old feelings and be grateful you can still see yours," Keyno motivated him to let go of the past. He didn't want Jabari to be like the fools who didn't respect and cherish their mama while they were alive. In the end, it always made them look like the idiot because you couldn't just walk and buy a mama out the nearest corner store. It was better to forgive and forget when it came down to the woman who birthed you."

"That's right. I see what you mean," Jabari agreed. He continued thinking about the idea until Keyno looked at him awkwardly. "Uhhh, ain't you missing school right now?"

"Yea, I got up late as hell. I got other shit to handle anyway." He brushed it off as if it meant nothing.

"Man, I remember when you ain't care about nothing but school. I'm talking about them young days where you ain't never speak to nobody and read books all day. Wishbone shirts and colored pencils." Keyno laughed.

"Damn, man. Don't bring that old stuff up. I hated those days. I had no control over my dress code, how healthy I ate, nothing. I damn sure ain't still watching Wishbone."

"I hope not. If so, you off the team." Keyno grabbed the blunt from him with a small chuckle.

Jabari knew that it was no cooler nigga than Keyno. It was the reason he stayed close to him and paid attention to every move and detail. In order to gain success, sometimes you had to follow until you were able to lead. Since being around his older idol, he placed paper in his pockets and always explained shit the correct way. If it was bad for a nigga, Keyno wouldn't allow you to do it unless you just didn't care about yourself. He was pushing for better when it came down to seeing Jabari do great with his life. The college life he saw inside of him was over and it was in his blood to follow the path of real taker. He just never seen a young one who was so ecstatic about taking over Cali one bank at a time. His eagerness and determination made Keyno want to ride in the backseat to see where his mind really wanted to go. He just didn't want them to wreck and burn along the way because of a vision he thought could work without assurance.

"So, when are you gonna be ready to handle this?" Keyno asked with a serious face.

"I say three days. I've been on my shit. I don't know why you worried cause I'm not gonna flop, bro."

"I never said you was, but I want you to be careful. These ain't no ordinary guns y'all gonna be running in there with. If anyone of them gets caught, it's an automatic ten years in the Feds. You say that shit good, so I can only speak off what you tell me. If this goes right, you'll be the leader to take us whereever you trying to go, young one. If it goes right, I'm with it." Keyno dapped him up before looking at his watch. "It's time for me to go handle my business for today. Listen, my house is your house. You break anything, you replace it like I was the one who broke it. Quick, fast, and in a hurry. Don't invite strangers over. Only yo lil team. This needs the be the time where y'all sitting down to lock in on what's ahead. It's serious, so be like Biggie, and treat that shit like ya first project," Keyno said before handing him a key, and walking back inside the crib.

Jabari thought about what he was envisioning for the crew after shit went accordingly the first time. Once Keyno was able to see that they were on point with the movements of what was at stake, the rest of the capers from then would be sweeter than candy on a red girl's kitty lips. It was time for a final sit down before the action began.

***
Hagginwood
Steven's House
3:14 P. M.

Leo and Teddy was slap boxing in the back yard while Steven sat to the side researching a few things for Jabari. It was now a mandatory roll call list for every bank in California. They crew wanted the smallest to the biggest. It was time to calculate, observe, and place their full energy into seeing exactly what it took, and how long would it be in order to swipe sixteen banks off the map as if they never existed.

Just when Steven was about to tell Leo and Teddy to check out what he found, Jabari was walking into his back yard. Being that his mother was working a double shift at the office, it left him ten free hours to do as he pleased with the guys.

Jabari walked past Leo and Teddy shaking his head. "Aye, can we focus? Y'all could of did all this shit when we were younger. We got bigger fish to fry," he said, sitting the bag in the ground next to him before taking a seat next to Steven at their outside wooden table. "What all did you find out?"

"I see that the software Leo has can manipulate their systems for one minute at the longest. That's all we need to get the drawers and leave back out. The alarms will be deactivated within that small period of time, but we have to be sure that there isn't any extra heroes inside. The police station sits exactly five minutes away which gives us a seventy-five second start on them before they can reach the bank and figure out what's going on," he answered confidently.

"So that means by the time they reach the bank, we should be halfway back to Hagginwood," Jabari said pointing at the Google map to be sure.

"Exactly. It's impossible for us to get caught. The only way the police could even get a glimpse of us is if they have new cameras that can speed up and flash ten light years ahead to catch me. We're gonna get away. Period," Steven assured as he kept typing.

"Perfect. Aye guys, chill for a minute and check this out," Jabari called out for Leo and Teddy to freeze their horse playing for a second.

Pausing their slight workout, they both walked over to the table and took a seat. "So wassup with it, Boss Man? What we doing?" Leo asked breathing heavily. He was energetic at the moment but knew that it was time to buckle down and hear out the plan thoroughly. Keyno sent them all a text to the burnout phones letting the crew know that if they were getting money together, the final decisions would go through Jabari before it was executed. The first bank job was in three days and he wasn't playing about shit being perfect.

"We moving out Monday morning. It's final. I got the layout. I got the plan. We move in, push the tellers away from the counter first. Being sure to watch out for ink patches inside of those fake ass bags they like to hand out during robberies. We're bringing our own. All the cash inside should be able to fit inside of y'all small backpack. We in there and out. I'll handle the security guard. He's big, but I got something that'll humble him down for sure. I have the guns. All I need is my team to understand what's at stake. Our lives. Our freedom. We must be serious and watching the time like a hawk on a mouse." Jabari nodded his head before picking up the bag off the floorboard next to him. Pulling out the four masks, he handed Steven one, then passed Teddy and Leo theirs.

"Wait. Hold up. Why the hell y'all got all the good ass Presidents and I'm stuck with fucking Hilary Clinton?" he said with agitation.

Steven was John F. Kennedy. Leo was George W. Bush, and Jabari was President Barack Obama.

"I bought you that one because you always acting like the bitch." He laughed through the mask.

"Fuck you, man. This old bitch is creepy and I'ma still lay something down whether I'm a freaky ass First Lady or a crooked ass President." He slid the mask over his face, trying to get the feel of it.

Jabari slid his mask back off and smiled. "We have the test, now let's knock it out. That way we can get to some big-league paper."

"Are you sure that everything is on point? Is there anything else we need to worry about?" Teddy asked curiously.

"Man, all you gotta do is show up and get money, fat boy. We got this shit in the bag. It's simple, and we're not gonna make it hard. We in that bitch and we out. Twenty minutes later, we should be eating some burgers and fries from the closest burger joint and heading back to Keyno's to divide that paper. Any questions?" Jabari asked looking at all three of them.

Silence passed through them all causing Jabari to stand up and clasp his hands together. "Good. I thought of us a name. It'll be easier than moving around California being friendly with every motherfucker we meet. We need some for the crew when we step. Like The City of Kings." He grinned looking up at Steven.

"Hell yeah. I like that," Leo added. He was sitting back nodding his head, listening harder than a muthafucka.

Steven gave him the thumbs up and Teddy slid the Hilary Clinton mask over his face giving a light shrug. "I'm horny babyyyyy. Let's be Kings around this bitch."

Jabari smiled knowing the next few months were about to shock the people horribly. They were gonna witness the new smooth criminals in town, and all limits for the law were now unrestricted.

* * *

Hagginwood
Ronald's House
7:35 P. M

Brandon walked out of his bedroom, bumping directly into Ronald coming in the house from work. Just from the way he came in staggering, you could tell he had gotten some of those cheap liquor shots like he did every Friday after getting that paycheck. His eyes was bloodshot red and Brandon was so focused on the cellphone in his hand that he'd forgotten to take off the clothes Jabari bought, so Ronald wouldn't trip.

After getting kicked out the house yesterday, Ronald took it upon himself to throw all the new clothes in the cubie can. Brandon went back and crept that shit right after he spotted his dad fall asleep later on after that. Just from the look on Ronald's twisted face, Brandon knew that it was too late to bust a U-turn. "Where in the fuck did you get those clothes? Cause it better not be the shit I threw in that hurbbie cubie." He sat down his work bag and folded his arms.

Brandon's remark was mumbled lower than his usual tone around the house. He couldn't even raise his head to look Ronald in the eyes. A hard-right fist rocked against his cheek sending him to the floor. He was now staring up at Ronald who was snarling like demon. "I said that you will not have that illegal ass shit in my house, negro. You can't hear, or you trying to play the tough guy role like your brother?"

Tears formed in Brandon's eyes from the heavy punch and he couldn't feel where the thick line of blood on his shirt was spilling from. Cradling his hands around his face, he whimpered, "How can you be mad because he bought me something? I didn't take or steal nothing."

"I wouldn't give a damn if you was in another state when it happened. You wearing it makes you just as guilty. Take it off now!" Ronald fumed.

"No man. I'm tired of you hitting on me. You never hit me in front of Jabari." Brandon continued to ball up as he shouted.

Ronald snatched off his thick leather belt with the quickness. Grabbing Brandon by his jeans, he nearly ripped them bitches in two. The hard lash across his back with the belt caused him to yell out in agony, "Ahhh!"

Ronald began to beat him unmercifully wherever he spotted skin. Kicking him in the rib cage. He slapped the belt across his chest, forcing him to cry louder. "Shut the fuck up, boy. You think you grown, huh?" Ronald was now raining his foot down repeatedly on his son's head forcefully. Ripping the Balenciaga shirt from Brandon's upper half, he tossed it across the room. "This is my house, nigga. You belong to me not the other way around. Now, tell ya bitch ass brother what I did and I'll bury you right next to him. Get up and get rid of it. Now!" Ronald yelled before storming out of the house.

Wiping the blood from the back of his head, Brandon stood up and tried to cover his naked body. His pants were split down the middle and his shirt was shredded to pieces. His brain was thumping with a sharp pain and before he could take one step, he crashed out against the floorboard face first.

* * *

Jumping in his car, Ronald mumbled to himself before smashing out of the parking lot. The disrespect of Brandon going behind his back for Jabari's word made him furious. He was pushing the pedal heading down to the store for another six back of beer before he snapped out and committed a murder. Jabari was filling his head with all that Black Lives Matter talk thinking that it would save him from an ass whooping. The shit wasn't happening under his roof, period. Brandon was only thirteen, and before he left the home to follow his brother's dumb ass footsteps, Ronald was prepared to body his ass and take him before he allowed the streets.

Pulling down into the corner store, he stepped out and his eyes landed on Blow standing outside of his Jeep Cherokee. His music was loud and he shuffled a small young chick around in his arms like he was the coolest nigga in the world. Ronald wanted to keep walking in the store, but just the fact of this young idiot being part of the reason for his son's dumb behavior, he decided to check that shit before it rubbed off on his youngest.

Walking over to him, Ronald folded his arms with that fake ass old chain gang press. "Aye, little nigga. I need to have a word with you."

Blow looked around as if he might have been talking to the trees or a nigga behind him. "I ain't got no crack, dad. Leave me the fuck alone. I'm busy," he said calmly before kissing his little fling.

Ronald moved a little closer. "Fuck that. This about my son, nigga. You and I need to speak little nigga."

Blow twisted up his face and moved the chick out of his way. "Nigga, who the fuck you supposed to be? I don't know yo son and I don't know you. Find somebody to safe to play with old head."

"Fuck all that young buck. Jabari and Brandon are my two sons. You and that nigga Kentavious are running around here playing tough, hurting people, and taking shit like y'all just some gorillas. Stay away from mines, nigga. Keep your money, your illegal ass ways, and all that shit far away from my kids. This is the warning, bruh." Ronald pointed a finger sternly with wide eyes.

Blow couldn't help but to laugh. "Nigga, you must be high. I don't fuck with yo bitch ass son anyway. That ain't my friend, nigga. Keyno fucks with them young ones, old man. I couldn't care less about you or them. Watch ya mouth and keep it pushing it like a broom across this parking lot before I spank you out here."

Ronald rolled up his sleeves slowly and the alcohol was still pumping through his veins like water spilling from an over flooded sink. At that moment, he wanted to hear one thing and judging from the shit that Blow was spitting, he wasn't about to switch it up to ease the tension.

"I'll beat you to death, young buck. You think you wanna see me since you trying to flex in front of this lil bitch. Back in my days of being in prison, you would have been a wash boy playing with OG's like me. Step in the box and I'll knock yo ass out." He pounded a fist on his chest heavily.

Blow's anger was ticking like a wall clock and fighting the big old ass nigga was surely out of the question. He heard stories about Ronald when he was younger, and supposedly he was the hood's nightmare. The nigga was still bench pressing two-fifty with ease, and he was thirty years older. Nodding for his young freak to get in the car. He looked back over to Ronald. "Check this big dawg. I don't know who you think I am, but you ain't in the eighties no more. This ain't yo block no more and this will be the day you die if you think about laying one finger on me. I'ma tell you one last time to walk off," Blow spat, dropping his right hand down beside his hip.

Kill was the trigger word which made Ronald move forward. His steps were quick and he cocked back to deliver a right haymaker. Blow peeped his movements too quick and pulled his weapon. The sight of the gun forced Ronald to freeze which was the worst mistake he could've made. The fire from the pistol was the last thing he seen before everything went black.

Boom!

Chapter 10
Keyno's House

It had been a few hours since Jabari left from around his aces. Shit was in motion and things were about to become more leveled out for the team once he placed the last pieces of his surprise puzzle together. The sound of his phone buzzing grabbed his attention from the laptop he was occupying. Reaching over to grab it, he answered while keeping his eyes glued to the screen. "Yeah?"

"Jabari, where are you?" Steven asked with a shaky tone.

"I'm at Keyno's spot. Why the hell you sound like that?" He continued to scroll down the long article about using high powered tools to enter some shit illegally.

"Because I saw Ronald leaving out of the house yelling to himself. He got in his car and swerved off pretty reckless. The front door was still cracked, so I went over to check on Brandon. Jabari, he was on the floor bleeding and unconscious. I think Ronald jumped on him pretty bad."

"What!" Jabari snapped standing up to his feet. The computer that was in his lap crashed to the floor.

"Yeah. The ambulance is here now, but I wouldn't recommend coming over here with a gun. The police are everywhere. I think they may be looking for Ronald."

"I'm on the way." Jabari hung up the call and jumped into his Jordan sneakers. Keyno stayed right in the hood, so Ronald's spot was less than five minutes away. The thought of him touching Brandon caused his skin to flare. Tossing a hoodie over his head, he grabbed his chrome 45, and struck out the front door running full speed. The warning about his brother was set the night he decided to leave Ronald's home, but he obviously took the shit lightly as if it was a game. Tonight was gonna be the moment Jabari showed him how serious he was about that statement.

The small run to the hood nearly had him out of breath, but he continued to dash across the streets and cars until he made his way past the corner store at the end of Ronald's block. The blue lights were flickering everywhere and he could easily count over sixty something people crowded out front being nosey, just to gossip later to the streets. That alone made him slow down and pace himself. He didn't need to be looking suspicious. He wasn't trying to alert the cops that he was about to go and shoot his father either.

Walking down in the hood further, he moved past a few small groups of people who stood around whispering. His movements stopped when he spotted Keyno standing behind the large crowd with a distraught face. Their eyes locked and just from the way he lowered his vision, Jabari could tell that something was seriously wrong. Walking over towards the crowded parking lot, Keyno reached his hands out to stop him. "Don't go over there, young one," his voice was crackly as if he was about to cry.

"Keyno, what's going on? What happened?" He tried to move his hand and look past him.

"Please Jabari. Don't go over there," he begged.

Spotting Ronald's car through all the shuffling citizens, Jabari's heartrate increased. Pushing Keyno's hand off him, he shoved through the people until he reached the front. The sight of his father laying on the pavement forced him to grow weak instantly. A bloody sheet was the only thing covering his face, and upper body. One of his work boots was lying next to him and the police was snapping pictures, while forensics rolled a line of caution tape around his vehicle. Pain wasn't the word he felt at the moment. His eyes fluttered trying to endure the sight, but it was critical.

Before his rage could release, Keyno placed a hand on his shoulder. "Please don't look at that shit, young one. I know it's hard, but I just wanna get you away from here right now. Please." He gave Jabari a look of sorrow, forcing his energy to settle. Tears streamed down his face, and it was actually the first time Keyno ever saw him show any emotion of being hurt.

"Who did this?" Jabari bit down on his bottom lip with a devastated expression.

"I'm not sure, young one, but we will find out. We have to go and check on Brandon because he's at the hospital. He's hurt and standing here will only make you want to do something that you will regret by morning. I promise I won't stop until we find out what the hell is going on." Keyno placed a hand over his heart to let Jabari know that he was definitely feeling his pain.

Refusing to stand weak for the man who caused him so much struggle, Jabari adhered to Keyno's words and walked off towards the truck. Climbing in the passenger seat, he closed the door and looked over to him. "I don't know who did this, but I will pay to find out. Ronald was some bullshit, but he was my father. I'm killing whoever was involved. Will you help me?"

Keyno took a second to think before answering the young bull. He could see the sincerity written in his eyes and the respect alone for Jabari was the reason he just couldn't deny him. "That's on my mother's life. I'll help."

The silence he gave forced Keyno to grab his shoulder lightly. "I promise. Don't second guess me. "

Jabari nodded and pulled the hoodie over his head, as Keyno pulled quickly off the block. The city was already having the pandemics of a government crisis, and now the animal behind the young, prudent mastermind was about to add another story for the headlines. That day caused Jabari's heart to turn beyond cold, and the gloves were officially sliding off for good.

* * *

Mercy General Hospital
Sacramento, California

Waiting outside in the family area of the hospital, Jabari's foot rocked back and forth thinking about the condition of his little brother. Keyno, Leo, and even Strawberry showed up to the hospital in order to show support after all the bullshit that occurred throughout the night. The sound in the little waiting room was lower than a creeping mouse. Everyone was expecting to hear the worse, after the disturbing shit with Ronald exploded all over the news. It was booming through the hood hard, and that shit tore a few people up. Not knowing to a lot of others, but back in the day, he was truly the man a young cat wanted to be. He was reckless. Had the money and cars, and always got what he wanted. That was until he caught his bid and was forced off to prison. No one knows the story on what happened inside Pelican Bay, but they did know he came home a so-called changed man.

Keyno and Jabari stood to their feet when the older white doctor stepped into the room.

"Tell us what's going on with no sugar coating, Doc." Jabari folded his arms impatiently. The silent movements in the hospital was stating to tweak him out.

"Well, it seems like he's gonna be okay. He got a little gash in the top of his head, but nothing life threatening. He obviously rushed to his feet after the assault and tried moving a bit too fast. We're prescribing him some medicine and he should be able to leave within the next hour," the doctor replied calmly before folding the chart in his hand.

"Thank God," Leo mumbled, releasing a deep breath. He knew that hearing anything other than that was going to result in Jabari probably losing his mind.

Jabari couldn't help but to thank the Supreme Being at that time. Brandon was all he had left. Looking up at the doctor, he shook his hand firmly. "Is it possible that I can go in and speak to him?"

"Sure. He's in the first room across the hall. I should have his release papers in a few." The doctor nodded before walking off.

Keyno patted Jabari's shoulder. "Go holla at lil bro. We're gonna head outside and wait in the truck. I know y'all need some privacy right now."

"Thanks, Keyno." Jabari walked off and headed across the hall.

Opening the room door, Brandon sat on the bed with his head hung low. A bandage was wrapped around the back of his head, but his spirit looked more crushed than anything.

Jabari moved over to him quickly and placed a hand under his head to lift it up. "What the fuck happened? Word for word."

Brandon sensed how tense his brother was and knew that lying wasn't about to fly anymore. "He wouldn't stop hitting me, Jabari." Tears instantly began to flood down his young face. "He came in drunk from work. I had the clothes on that you bought me. I forgot to take them off and he beat me. He wouldn't stop hitting me, man," Brandon cried, releasing the truth.

"Why didn't you run?"

"I couldn't. He hit me before I could. He's been doing it since we've moved in with him. He said if I ever told you that he would kill me."

"Tell me what, Brandon? You telling that this man has been beating on you. Is that what you're telling me?" Jabari looked at him with a heated expression.

Brandon stood to his feet and removed his shirt. Turning around. Jabari gasped from the deep and dark whips that climbed his back. Hundreds of deep scars covered his spine from the months of abuse Ronald unleashed upon him.

Jabari shed a tear, and slowly turned him around. "Why didn't you ever tell me, Brandon? Why?"

Brandon cried harder. "Because Ronald said he was gonna kill you if I did. He was scared of you, Jabari."

Wrapping Brandon up for a hug, he quickly calmed him. "Just be easy. It's over now. I'll never give anybody else the chance to hurt you ever again. I promise."

"Jabari?"

"Wassup, young one?" He looked down at his younger brother.

"Is Ronald really dead?"

Even though his anger was boiling at a thousand degrees for Ronald, he still refused to parade about the death of their father. He hoped his ass was punished in the afterlife about the conditions of the way he mistreated Brandon, but giving the initiative for another to take his life instead of the higher being was definitely not about to be accepted.

"Yeah. He's gone, but don't celebrate. We're not gonna rejoice about that because he was taken away by the hands of a human. Just know that you're safe now, and I'll never allow another person to harm you. Let's go." Jabari placed an arm around his shoulder.

Walking him to the front desk for his release papers, pain felt so different when it was caused by the hands of your own blood. Love was only a word used for advantage and it truly was hard to find real motherfuckas who actually gave two shits about someone other than themselves. That shit closed Jabari's heart for a new chapter, and it wasn't a sweet one. First things first. He was gonna find the one who caused Ronald's death, and after that, force Sacramento to beg for his mercy.

Chris Green

Chapter 11

It was around seventy thirty the next morning when Jabari cracked his eyes to the gloomy sky. Rising from the bed, he placed his feet on the floor and walked over to the window. Staring out at the cloudy scenery reminded him of the dreadful tragedy they suffered with yesterday. After getting all the rest he could, it still didn't decrease his anger from what was currently on their hands. The life as they knew of it was officially over, and Jabari was literally gonna have to become a provider quicker than he thought.

Staring back at the large picture of Nelson Mandela, he knew that suffering wasn't the word for the struggle he went through. Spending twenty-seven years in the prison of a country and coming home to be the president was a true testimony. Pain and losses came within that journey, and it surely didn't stop the best from occurring afterwards. Money was the new motive, and power was the next goal.

Walking out of Keyno's large guest bedroom, he trailed smoothly to the living room and spotted the entire crew present. Leo, Teddy, Blow, and Keyno. Brandon sat in a chair like he was interested in whatever Keyno was speaking about. Everyone seemed to freeze and look up once they realized Jabari was up.

"Wassup, young one? We've been waiting for you to rise." Keyno nodded humbly.

Jabari tapped Brandon's shoulder. "Aye, head in the room while we all talk. You shouldn't be out here anyway. I'll take you out for breakfast in a second."

"Okay." Brandon stood to his feet and disappeared to the back of Keyno's home.

Jabari rested back in the chair and looked around again. "Where is Steven?"

"We don't know. His mom is doing something across town with him, but he said that he'll be prepared by morning if he still needs to assist," Leo answered.

Jabari nodded and rubbed his hands together. "Cool."

"I was just in here telling the guys how y'all should head back. The expressway is exactly four blocks on the backside of the bank. You would have to make a left off that street and drive straight out," Keyno clarified.

"I already got the map down to a science. I'm from Old Sacramento, bro. Not to mention, Steven is an expert with driving. He's gonna get us out of there before anyone could notice what's going on," Teddy said with confidence.

"How you positive? Anything is possible to screw the fuck up when you speaking about taking off a bank. He might get nervous and wreck. Then what?" Keyno smirked.

"Like I said, I ain't never seen a nigga drive better than Steven. I can bet you whatever you want. Our crew has been getting down on sweet shit. We might make it seem like we green, Keyno, but we ain't the average seventeen-year olds. I know he can pull it off," Teddy assured.

"He's not lying, Keyno. Steven is a beast. The main deal is about us getting in there and out. We got one minute to handle that business and that's exactly what I was about to speak on. I'm not playing with this shit. If we raising up on this level, it's full throttle from here on out. Fuck plotting anything else. We got the plan down and we heading out tomorrow. Whoever ain't ready will be exposed. This is my team and we running this by ourselves, Keyno. After we break even, the next move will be on y'all." Jabari looked at him, and Blow.

"Well, I guess there's nothing else to talk about. Where we eating?" Leo asked wanting to drop the negative talk. In his head, it was gonna go be perfect. It was the only way to build their accounts, and the moment was finally here.

"Fuck it. Let's get Strawberry's ass over here to fix us up a real Kings meal." Keyno stood up and lit his plump Kush blunt.

Jabari stood to his feet. "Cool. I'm gonna make a quick run somewhere. I'll be back in an hour." He headed for the room to change clothes. The time was now seven-thirty-five and the morning was moving slow like he needed it to. It was the best time to move without being seen.

* * *

Cynthia's Cake Bakery
2376 Fair Oaks Boulevard

Victoria moved around the shop, wiping the tables and cleaning the counters. Her beautiful long hair was pulled back into a large bun, and she was dressed in a tight fitting black one-piece jumper. Her apron gave her the sweet wife's appearance, and her black lipstick complimented her sexy Italian culture. Hearing the bell signal over the entrances she looked up to see Jabari standing in front of her. The presence of him alone forced her heart to flutter with love. Jabari was eyeing her as if he wanted to wrap his arms around Victoria and kiss her passionately. He moved slowly over to her and removed the black hoodie from his head. The smell of his Calvin Klein cologne floated from Jabari's Puma sweat suit. "Hey," he said in a low tone. His eyes roamed her body, and he didn't care about her personal space at the time.

"Hi handsome." She reached in for a hug.

The lovely aura he felt once she grabbed him was like no other. It was as if all his troubles could just disappear from her delicate touch. He couldn't help but to press his nose against her neck. She was perfection and beauty wrapped in one. That small moment was so calming that he didn't want it to end. "I was thinking about you and decided to stop by."

Victoria smiled. "That's why I gave you my number, so you wouldn't have to think."

Leading him over to a table, she sat down beside him. His smile was glowing, but she could tell that his happiness wasn't one hundred percent. "What's bothering you?" She gazed into his eyes sincerely.

"What makes you think something is bothering me?"

"Because you usually smile the entire time you move. I can sense it on you," she replied.

Trying to straighten his posture, he shook off the bad buzz and flashed her a big one to lighten the mood. "It's really nothing. I just was pretty tired getting up so early, but I had to come speak to you," he lied.

"Is everything okay?"

"Yes. I was actually gonna be completely honest with you. I know that I've never gotten the chance to know you deeply, neither have we ever connected as one. I'm not good with asking girls out on the date thing, but I am good with being a provider and protector." Jabari grabbed Victoria's hand gently and looked into her eyes.

"What are you saying, Jabari?"

Her mother, Cynthia, was behind the counter listening with a close ear. The protection of their family was beyond serious and she could tell what answer was coming next just from his first statement.

"I wanna be here for you and hopefully grow as more than just a friend. I wanted to know if you would be my girlfriend. I swear that I don't have any ill plans or any other women. I'm a good man, and I'm only building a path for a family who never has to worry about the future. I would like to start that journey with you." He shrugged after releasing what was on his mind.

"Please just say yes," Cynthia pleaded with a huge smile.

"Mamaaa!" Victoria blushed waving her off. The excitement was glowing all over her and she couldn't help but to accept Jabari's request. It was rare where a man would ask you so fast to be his woman, especially when the part of getting to know each other wasn't established yet. It was also the only way she could keep a track on him.

Leaning forward, she kissed his lips gently. "As long as you don't disappear for months at a time like you usually do. You can have me forever."

His heart couldn't pump at the moment from her sweet tender kiss. He could taste the winter fresh gum that she was chewing on a few minutes before he entered the store and her soft hands was cradling his cheeks like he was a newborn baby.

"Thank you, Lord. My familia can live on. I need grandbabies." Cynthia pointed at them both before walking back into the kitchen.

Jabari couldn't help but laugh. It felt great to have the acceptance of her mother so quickly. No man was ever able to slide in an Italian race without being blessed by the father, so he knew that it would be coming very soon. "Now that I've gotten the hard part out the way, I wanna make sure that I'll be the best to you. I know that your mom works hard in the shop, and I want to work twice as hard to ensure that you're okay."

Victoria nodded but lowered her vision slightly. "Jabari, my mom tries, but sometimes trying isn't enough. We've had this shop in our family for over thirty years, and now it's about to end."

"What do you mean?"

"She can't manage the payments on the bakery and they have stacked up tremendously. It's getting closed down by next month if we can't catch up. It looks like I'm going to be the one taking care of her if we don't get it resolved," she said with a look of doubt.

"What do you mean closed down?" Jabari questioned.

"I mean shut down. The lease of this building was under my father's name, and the business just doesn't make the money that it was making before my dad passed a few months back. Since then, me and my mama have been struggling to maintain the doors to stay open. We barely get any customers."

Jabari looked out the window of Cynthia's shop pondering on what Victoria was saying. It was clear that they needed help, and it was also crystal that the government was ready to come seize their property if they weren't able to come off the requested money from the state.

"How much does it cost?"

Victoria huffed as if the number was impossible. "Too much."

"Hey, don't stress on me right now. I said how much does it cost?" Jabari asked again with a confident tone.

"Roughly thirty-seven thousand dollars." Victoria tooted her lips like the number left a salty taste in her mouth.

Nodding, he leaned over and kissed her gently. "I'm gonna help. I will be back down here tomorrow. Make sure you keep mama here a little late. Maybe til nine or ten. I will come back and give you whatever I can," he assured and kissed her fingers after.

"Okay." She smiled feeling her thighs, and womanhood tingle from his firm touch.

Standing up from the chair, he hugged her tightly and placed the throw away phone he purchased in her hand. "Hold this. I'm the only one who will call that number, so if you see it ring, answer." He held her hips and kissed her cheek once more before quickly leaving out of the bakery.

Victoria turned around to see Cynthia standing behind the counter with a smile. "I like him, Vicki. He will protect you for sure. Your father always told me how to spot if a man is worthy enough to be family. He's a keeper."

"I believe you, mama. He said that he wants to help you with the shop," she said with excitement.

"Let's pray and hope so. Even if he can't the thought counts for any person who tries and makes the effort to help us. I would rather see you happy, princess. It was your Papa's dream." She smiled before continuing to sweep the floor.

Victoria kept her eyes on Jabari as he walked down the street. She knew that over the years of watching him come in and out of the store that he held a unknown significance, but now those deep thoughts she envisioned was turning into reality.

Chris Green

City of Kingz

Chapter 12

Arriving back to Keyno's house. Jabari entered the front door and greeted everyone with a nod. Strawberry was caked under Keyno. Blow, Teddy and Leo was sharing a blunt while playing a hand of cutthroat. Brandon was sitting at the table with them as if he really knew what the fuck he was doing. Instead of slapping him across the head, he decided to handle business first. Tapping Keyno on his leg, Jabari looked at Strawberry's big booty self, eyeing him down. "Hey, Berry. You mind if I holla at Keyno for a second?'

"Yep, I do mind. You ain't gave me a hug, boy. Ain't spoke or nun. Show me you ain't got no attitude." She stood up and held open her arms. Keyno shrugged with a smile and headed for the kitchen, leaving him to deal with her over aggressive ass. Reaching in for a hug, she placed one of his hands on her soft butt and whispered into his ear, "I wanna fuck you, lil boy. I know you be seeing me trying to give you this pussy." She rolled her tongue across his ear.

Nobody was obviously paying attention because she damn sure grabbed a hand full of his dick before letting him go.

"You gotta stop being so uptight, Jabari. We're all family, baby boy." Strawberry winked before walking to the back. Her booty was so hypnotizing that she turned Teddy's head like an owl.

"Damnn that girl got too much turkey back there. I don't think I got enough mayo for all that," he joked, making the entire table laugh.

Jabari brushed off the disturbing image in his mind and headed for the back porch where Keyno was rolling a giant Backwoods. "Young one. What's good?"

Moving over to the table, he sat down across from him. "You need to check Strawberry, Keyno. She's a little to touchy, bro."

"Man, I can't control what that girl does. She ain't my wife and that's just the way Strawberry is. She's a stripper, Jabari. Get you some pussy and lighten up, Jabari. You make me think you a virgin, lil nigga." Keyno laughed.

Jabari's words shortened after Keyno's comment. "That ain't the point. I just want her to show you some respect. She's here as your guest."

Keyno lit the blunt and passed it to Jabari. "Lil bro, she's only a friend. If you don't want her grabbing on you, then tell her. She obviously likes you. I'm still talking about this virgin shit though. Have you ever had some pussy, young one?"

Hitting the weed, Jabari lowered his head. "No, I haven't, but that ain't where my mind is at my nigga. I don't care about all that, plus I just got with a girl who I been wanting for a minute. So pussy isn't a problem."

Keyno broke out into a fit of laughter. "Nigga, I knew it. No wonder you be punching fools out in school and ready to lay shit down. You need some ass, Jabari."

"Man, come on Keyno. You too loud. I didn't come out here to speak about this." He started to get aggravated.

"Cool, but how you gonna please this girl that you got now if you don't know what you're doing, young one? You're getting some pussy today. Period," Keyno said waving him off.

"Look man, I'm speaking about this mission tomorrow. We have a big job ahead of us, but I need to know that you got my back if shit was to go left," Jabari said with a serious face.

"What do you mean?"

"I mean if I happen to get caught or die trying to provide for mines, I need you to look out for my brother. He's all I got, Keyno."

"Jabari, that's the last thing you need to worry about. You ain't going nowhere, lil bro. This is our life, but we also have steps that we follow. Nothing can stop that but the man above, and if he does it, that means it was meant to be."

"But what if it doesn't happen like we plan, Keyno?"

"Then we regroup, and plan again. The first rule is always the same. We don't panic. The next is always have a backup. We're smart niggas, not dumb. The third is never doubt. We're winners also which means doubting isn't in our vocabulary, young one. Stay focused and let's eat. This what you wanted, right?" Keyno asked before passing him the blunt.

Jabari couldn't do anything but nod. The pandemonium that occurred the night before forced him to see that losing Brandon could happen in a blink of an eye if he wasn't more careful. "Yeah. It is."

"Cool." Keyno stood up with a smile. "Now, about this no pussy thing. You about to go inside, hit the shower, and I'm gonna tell Strawberry to come holla at you." He grinned.

"I don't know about that Keyno. That's not how I'm rocking, bro. All these niggas don't need to know my business."

"Man, listen. I'm about to take Brandon and the fellas out for a good time. Get in that damn shower, and

Strawberry is gonna keep you company while were gone. You trust me, right?"

Jabari took another toke of the weed. "Yeah, Keyno."

"Well stop acting crazy. Head in there and let ya big brother operate this train. This is mandatory." He smiled before walking back inside.

Knowing that it was too late to get out of the drama he just mixed himself into, Jabari hit the marijuana as hard as he could and headed back into the crib. Strawberry sat on the couch with a wide smile, as Keyno rounded up the crew to head out.

Jabari made his way inside the master bathroom and closed the door behind him. Taking a deep breath. He turned on the hot water for the shower and stripped out of his clothes. Once the steam began to fill the air, he stepped inside and grabbed a bar of soap from the rail. Placing his head under the water, Jabari allowed it to calm his nervousness. The sound of the door opening forced him to crack his eyes. He wanted to turn around, but the secret exposed by Keyno made that shit kinda hard. Once the shower curtain slid back. He turned his head to see Strawberry standing before him fully naked. Her eyes rotated down to his manhood and she couldn't help but to grin with joy.

"Hey big boy. Can I join you?"

"Uhhh," Jabari stuttered nervously, while viewing her seductive body. Her caramel colored nipples were perfect with the for the c-cup breast on her body. Her plump ass was round and jiggled lightly as she stepped over into the shower with him. Jabari faced her when she moved closer. Her hand moved down to his dick stroking with expertise.

"Damn that shit is huge. What you bout to do with all this?" She asked seductively before placing a nasty kiss on his lips.

Jabari's chest rose with adrenaline and he placed his back against the wall. Strawberry licked her lips while stroking his meat back and forth. "Keyno said that you needed me to show you a few things. I just want you to relax, daddy." She squatted down and placed his large piece down her throat. Bobbing her head back and forth, she gagged lightly and snatched him out of her mouth. "Ooohh goodness." She slobbed before rubbing a hand across his stomach.

Jabari closed his eyes and could feel his chest turning knots from whatever the fuck Strawberry was doing to him. His sex experience was on the floor, but she was clearly making an example of whatever Keyno asked her to do.

Strawberry's sexy black hair was getting wet and her titties bounced around as she handled the business with that tongue action. "Look at me, Jabari," she moaned before taking him back down her throat.

Opening his eyes, he witnessed her freaky side taking over. Her tongue glided across the head of his member forcing the freaky sucking sound to get louder.

Jabari felt that he would faint from the feeling that shit was giving him. Placing a hand on her head, he tried to slow Strawberry down, but she slapped his shit down. Speeding up her pace, she tried to deep throat his cock forcing him to bust quickly. His body trembled like a small child, and she could tell that he enjoyed it from the way his eyes rolled in satisfaction. Making sure to clean up her mess, she allowed the water to roll over her breast and stood back up to look him in the eyes. "Did that feel good, lil daddy?" Strawberry grinned.

All Jabari could do was nod. He was in a trance from her nastiness, and now her fine ass was starting to look like a real treat.

"Good. Come with me." She grabbed his hand and pulled him out of the shower. He couldn't help but to watch her ass rock back and forth. She didn't have a blemish on her body and Jabari's shit was stiffer than a muthafucka wondering what was next.

Entering the room, she moved slowly to the bed and bent over on all fours. Her ass arched, giving him a full view of her pink sweet candy. "Don't mash all that dick in me, boy. Take your time." She looked back at him, rubbing her clit in anticipation.

Moving up behind her, Jabari guided himself inside, but of course she had to help him get to the right spot. Once he felt the soft wetness soak his piece, he melted like a candy bar over a hot stove. Strawberry rotated her hips, letting his dick fill her up slowly.

"Sss. Get in there, lil daddy."

Not knowing his own strength, he mashed his shit into her kitty forcing her to slightly jump. "Damn boy! Not that hard. You gotta be easy. You ain't no little kid down there," she panted.

"I'm sorry." He was breathing like he could nut at any second.

"It's okay. Grab my hips and pump slow. Match my rhythm and take your time," she coached him.

Exhaling deeply, he followed her instructions and locked on to her hips. He was feeding her the dick kindly, but the sensational feeling was forcing him to slide in deeper.

"Yesss Jabari. Just like that. Slap my ass, daddy," she moaned before tossing her booty back lightly.

Giving her a light slap on the right butt cheek, he bit his bottom lip and began to lose control. Rubbing her ass with both hands. He spread her cheeks, watching his dick fill her up. His slow pumps began to speed up and become deeper, forcing Strawberry to slightly run. "Shittt!" She cringed from his length. The young nigga was packing and her pussy was speaking all types of foreign languages while that dick slammed inside her walls.

Slapping her ass forcefully, Strawberry looked back at Jabari handling that business. He was sliding in her shit with ease, and the way he dug in had her creaming on that dick like it was her last orgasm. For him to be a virgin, he felt like he was in a bitch's tummy. It was sad to say, but no man was able to make her run from the dick. But this young nigga's shit was a little too fat for her kitty."

"Jabariii-ii, slow down. It hu-rrtss." Strawberry held her mouth open feeling her next nut coming quickly.

"Shut up," he leaned down, whispering in her ear. "You said this what you wanted."

Now that Strawberry was on her stomach, she couldn't move and he wasn't being merciful with that wood. He was big enough to slide in and out that pussy with ease. She tightened her ass cheeks for him to slow down, and he still didn't stop.

"Fuckk, daddyy. I can feel that shittt!" she whined in a low tone.

The tables had officially turned and her stomach was now feeling like it was about to pop with his dick pumping inside her. Grabbing ahold of the sheets tightly, she bit down on a small piece and prayed that he would cum soon. His strokes grew heavier and harder, and now her ass was clapping against his stomach forcefully. Releasing himself inside of her guts, he laid on her back and kissed it gently.

"Thank you," was all he could say while kissing her ass and back repeatedly.

Panting heavily, Strawberry rolled over and pulled him down next to her. "You're on punishment, nigga." She poked his chest with her finger.

"What did I do?" He smiled, wrapping an arm around her.

"Nigga, that third leg down there that you just tried to kill me with. If you can't go lighter, yo lil big dick ass will not be getting no more ass lessons from me." She pecked lips and climbed out of the bed. "I'm going to get back in the shower."

"Okay," Jabari said while resting back on the bed.

Before Strawberry exited the room, she stopped. "Uhhh, rule number two. After giving a bitch a dose of some shit like that, when a woman says she's finna get in the shower, you should automatically join her." She smiled before walking out with her ass rocking hard.

Feeling his chest thump in excitement, he crawled out of the bed naked and headed directly behind her. Getting to the bathroom, he walked inside and closed the door behind him.

Chapter 13

The Next Morning
9:15 A. M.
West Armor Bank - 1610 Arden Way

Sitting directly across the street from their mission, Leo fumbled with his laptop nervously trying to trigger the system of the bank. Their takeoff was in less than four minutes, and he still had yet to power down the alarm and lights through his hacking program. Steven sat in the front seat with his John. F. Kennedy mask pulled over his face. Looking back at Leo, he snapped his fingers. "Try rebooting the program and powering it down through a different system on the app. It's like a cellphone. Sometimes you have to catch different channels in order for of to work."

"Man, whatever the fuck you gotta do to make it work." Teddy nudged him. "We got less than four fucking minutes."

"I'm trying, just chill the fuck out." Leo sweated lightly while tapping on the keys of his laptop for dear life.

Jabari sat quietly in the front passenger seat with his Barack Obama mask pulled down. The Heckler & Koch 48 assault rifle was clutched tightly in his hand, and he was staring through the bank's window, prepared to jump out whenever he spotted the sign to move in.

Steven glanced at his watch again. "We're down too three minutes."

Just as the words came out his mouth, Leo snapped his finger. "Got it bitch."

The West Armor Bank quickly grew pitch black inside giving them the clarification that it worked. "Go, Steven now!" Jabari shouted.

Mashing the gas, he cut straight through the intersections like a smooth professional and slid into the parking lot of the bank. Pulling directly in front of the doors, Jabari jumped out first with his gun aimed in front of him. Teddy was next, followed by Leo. Entering the building the security guard never seen what was coming until Jabari whacked him across the head. "Get the fuck on the ground now! Everybody get down!"

The lights made it nearly impossible to see, but the small sun ray coming through allowed him to see the three of them dressed in tailor-made suits with Presidents' masks on their faces.

Leo moved quickly over to the tellers pointing his gun towards them. "Back the fuck up from the drawer! Back up," he said hopping over the counter like a lemur. He wasted no time pulling the bag from his neck and taking all the cash from the first teller's drawer.

Teddy aimed his AK-47 at all the citizens that laid against the floor with their heads covered. He moved around tapping their pockets. removing cellphones, and wallets.

Jabari stared down at the guard who was leaking from the back of his head. He was biting down on his jaw as if he wanted to buck and be a hero, but the large weapon in his hands caused him to think twice.

"Just be easy, old man, and I'll be out of your hair in a second. We got one minute!" Jabari shouted while glancing at the watch on his wrist.

Leo continued moving, taking every coin out of the bank tellers' counters until they were all empty. Zipping up the large duffle, he tossed it back across his back. "I'm good!" he said, heading straight for the entrance.

Teddy made sure to collect every cell and even a Rolex off a man's wrist who was laying in the floorboard with the rest. "Me too, baby. I'm so horny right now! Whoo!" He licked his tongue through the Hilary Clinton mask at a fast pace.

Jabari removed the gun from the guards hip and anything else he could use for a weapon. Backing up to the entrance, he spoke his peace before leaving, "Thank you all for your cooperation, and pleased remember that you fucked up voting for Donald Trump as your president. Black America." He aimed his gun before running out of the door. By the time. they reached the car and smashed off, the lights inside of the bank was shuffling back on, and the alarm system started to slowly reboot.

Steven mashed the gas and headed out of the parking lot like a bat out of hell. He maneuvered through traffic to reach the designated backstreet, which would lead them straight for the expressway.

Teddy snatched his mask off with excitement. "I told you, baby! I fucking told y'all niggas!" He shook Leo's shoulder with excitement.

"We did that shit." Leo smiled after sliding his mask upon to breathe a little better.

"We ain't celebrating yet. Get back to our side of town, stop to get some burgers and fries, and let's go show Keyno and them how the real City of Kingz do this shit," Jabari said, whipping the new throwaway phone out of his pocket.

* * *

Sitting on the couch with Strawberry next to him, Keyno smoked a blunt of blue cheese Kush and opened his phone screen after the notification ringtone sounded off. Reading the message from Jabari to himself, he jumped to his feet and began to search the living room.

"Boy, what the hell is wrong with you?" Strawberry jumped from his reaction.

"Where is the remote?" He tossed around the pillows on the couch until he spotted that motherfucker. Turning the TV on, he went directly to the news station.

"This is news reporter, Brandy Williams, going live for *Channel 2 News* giving you the story about what just occurred over on Ardens Way at the West Armor Bank. Apparently, three masked gunmen ran into the place and robbed the entire building with large assault rifles. One of the victims stated that they were jacked by former Presidents of the United States. The lights were somehow blown out for a minute or two, and these guys came in and cleared the tellers' boxes and safe out for over one-hundred thousand dollars. Investigators are on the scene blocking the entire area off until we can locate an identity on these suspects, but there is no further information at this moment. What do you have to say about this terrible situation, Eric?"

"Ohhh shittt!" Keyno smiled from ear to ear before pulling on his blunt.

* * *

Heather's ass clapped back gently against Blow's dick. He couldn't help but to slap that lil soft motherfucker watching it jiggle back and forth. Rubbing his rough hands up and down her smooth back, he pounded inside her as the sweat began to drip from his forehead.

"Dump that dick in me, baby… Sssss. Stick that shit!" Heather crooned with delight. She was looking back into his eyes knowing that shit enticed him to the max.

Sliding out of her warm kitty, he stroked his piece and laid back gently on the bed. "Get on top of this motherfucker, girl. You know wassup," he ordered, ready to get back between them slippery lips.

Doing as she was told, Heather turned around to give him a full view of her back shot. Squatting down in his dick, it slid in with ease, forcing her kitty to poot in satisfaction."

"Damn just like that ma," Blow grunted as she started to quake that ass up and down on his manhood. Her pussy was soaking wet, not to mention, she was liable to jump off him and squirt at any giving minute. Heather's shit was tight like a mitten and she damn near made him cum every time she bounced on that shit. She was the type that lost control when it came to sex. She didn't mind sucking dick until you bust and she damn sho knew how to talk freaky as fuck to a nigga while in that bed.

Plowing his dick in her harder, he could feel his nut about to come.

"Beat this shit, nigga. I'm nutting all ova that dick, daddy," Heather moaned loudly. The mood was great. The morning sun came out of the sky giving them a great view of the rise through her bedroom window. Right when she was catching her second orgasm, his cellphone began to ring.

"God damn, Blow, answer that shit. That's the third time. Is that yo other bitch?" She climbed off him with an attitude.

"Girl shut the hell up. It ain't no other female." He reached over for the Galaxy touchscreen on her floor. Picking it up, he spotted Keyno's number and answered, "Nigga is it urgent?" Blow shouted.

"Nigga power the fuck down. Turn on the news. Pronto," Keyno said before hanging up.

Blow waved his hand around to Heather. "Turn on the news real quick, hurry up."

Following his orders, she snatched up the remote aggressively and flicked on the flat screen television. The fifty-inch LG came alive speaking about the smooth bank robbery that ook place today. Blow reached for his boxers, sliding them on before sitting in front of the TV. Reading the headlines, he slammed a hand on his knee. "Damn!

Boy, what's wrong? You act like a motherfucker died."

"I gotta go. I'll slide back later on when I finish up this business with Keyno."

Heather smacked her lips with annoyance. "You always on the move. You know damn well my daddy might pop up at any time. He's a cop, nut head." She snatched up her shorts, sliding them on swiftly.

"Fuck yo daddy. He be bugging every time he see me, but never say shit to Keyno. It's time to start sharing the respect around this town." Blow grabbed his car keys in a rush.

"Ain't no respect with that old man. My brother was shot a few months back out there in yo neighborhood. He don't like none of y'all Hagginwood niggas. Don't come over here if you don't call first, Blow. I'm serious." Her facial expression said that she wasn't joking.

"Whatever. Just make sure you know who running this shit, lil mama. You got me, so don't worry about all that other miscellaneous shit." He kissed her lips before walking out of the bedroom.

Moving through the nice crib, he walked out of the front door and jumped in the front seat of his Jeep. Turning the stereo up to the max, Drake's hit song "5AM in Toronto" boomed through the speakers. The thought of Jabari's caper going as planned was sweet. Now it was time to work his move and get in where he fit in. Sacramento was about to come off that shit big time, and he had the right young and dumb lil ones to do it with him. Smiling, he smashed off mumbling three words, "Lights, cameras, action."

City of Kingz

Chapter 14

45 minutes later
Keyno's House

"I'm telling you, man, that shit was beyondddd sweet!"
Teddy clapped his hands loudly. Picking up a handful of
fries, he shoved them in his mouth and wiggled a finger at
Keyno. "I told you that Jabari was a mastermind."
"Yeah. I'm still curious on how y'all jammed so damn
hard. This is some new profiling for the team. If we can
keep this shit booming correctly, we can be rich in no
time," Keyno replied while thumbing through the cash that
was sitting on his glass kitchen table.

"This isn't shit compared to what we can do. I'm
shooting for the big leagues with this thing. We can
accumulate more if we switch it up as we go, but the team
is solid. Now, the next move is on y'all." Jabari raised his
hands in the air as if his job was done.

Brandon crept from the backroom peeking around the
corner and gasped seeing the large payday in front of his
older role models. Of course, being caged behind the walls
would make your mind oblivious to the street life, but now
that he and Jabari were on their own, he was getting his
first sight of the law breaking crooks in training.

"Okay, so y'all got away with this little bitty ass vault.
What's next? Cause now I want in." Blow's smile curved
in like the Joker.

"That little bitty ass count is plus a hundred thousand."
Keyno flipped through the last stack of bills with a grin.

"I snatched open every fucking handle I seen." Leo
laughed, slapping hands with Teddy in excitement.

"It was common sense. All we needed was the shutdown from Leo's system to crash the banks database. It powered down, giving us the perfect chance to strike. It was easy, if I should say," Steven chimed in before his small TracFone rang off loudly. Quickly checking it, he viewed his mother's name and tapped Jabari's shoulder. "I gotta check in with the old lady to keep her lungs young. Just hold my portion, and I'll be through later to pick it up." He quickly grabbed his book bag and stood up from the chair.

"Come back," Jabari said with a straight face. "You know I need to see how this is about to go."

"Trust me. I'll be back in a swift like mama would say." He smiled before leaving out the front door on foot.

"Okay guys. We're at a hundred and six thousand in total. That's twenty-five stacks for all of y'all. I'll cap the six for y'all using the guns." Keyno stood up and threw a pile of money on Jabari's lap. "Y'all young ones did it. Fucking Jackpot!"

"Yeah, yeah. We need to be plotting on what's next," Blow butted in.

"Easy. We all got a lot of shit ahead of us. Twenty-five racks is a lot for me. I still got cash stashed. This was only a test. I just wanted to show you and Keyno that we can show up and succeed. The community can use this paper because it's bigger things I wanna do." Jabari stood up, patting Blow's shoulder lightly.

Leo's tall ass flexed his cut in the air like it was a degree certificate from Yale University. "True, plus we got graduation approaching quickly. We gotta skip that, and I'll be good to go."

"He's right," Keyno cut in. "Get this diploma and let's get some true cake."

Jabari nodded his head knowing that shit was true. He was all Brandon had now that Ronald was gone. It was all so crazy to him because Blow paid for the entire funereal. It shocked the hell out Jabari, especially when he did it through Keyno's face. That was a true blessing for the family in Ronald's family name, but unfortunately, he wouldn't be attending whatever they planned. The handling of his little brother would never be forgotten, but merely forgiven. The gift was the payment of his burial for whoever wished to show their respect, and that was it.

"We plan. We rise. I mean on some City of Kingz shit. After graduation, we strike and I mean big loads." Jabari smiled.

"Good, because you're taking lead. You got in, now show us what's next." Keyno folded his arms with a straight face.

Thinking about Victoria, Jabari smiled. "I gotta handle something real quick. Keyno, can you take me down to the bakery on Fair Oaks?"

"Now?'

Teddy stuffed all his cash in a small knapsack. His grin was a muthafucka. "Look, I'm just being real. I'm about to ball out with my shit. The mall. Old Sacramento is my legendary stories nigga. I'ma about to fuck a freak and dress up real neat."

"It's settled. I'll get up with y'all later. Me and Keyno need to discuss some stuff, and I'll head out to handle some small business to proceed on with my future. We taking over from there." Jabari rubbed his hands together.

* * *

Cynthia's Bakery

10:00 P.M.

The night sky was dark as death and the police was lurking on patrol like an officer of the law died around that bitch. Crazy thing is they really wanted to know what occurred at their bank today. Money and people were distraught, but the news media wanted to know one thing. Who were the criminal behind the quick get away?

"I'm right here, so handle your business," Keyno said slumping down in the seat with his big ass gun cocked.

"It'll be a second, Keyno. This means something to me."

"And you ain't gotta explain yourself to me." Lowering his Kings snapback over his eyes. "Go ahead."

Jabari closed his pea coat and slid a black skull cap on his head, stepping out into the windy night. He looked both ways to be sure of his surroundings before crossing the street. You could still see the open sign in Cynthia's Bakery's glass door. A few lights were still shining, giving him the indication that Victoria trusted his words.

Jabari entered the front door. Cynthia was sitting at a table with her in a deep conversation and their faces looked as if they were starting to doubt. Once he crossed the threshold of her mother's shop, Victoria stood to her feet with a curious grin. Walking over to Jabari, she gave him a tight hug. "It's okay if you couldn't have it. I know that me and my mom aren't your problem."

Ignoring her statements. He kissed her just like Strawberry told him. His new aggressiveness gave her a slight moistness between her thighs. "I didn't mean to show up so late." He rubbed on her arms to spread a light relief. Grabbing her hand, he walked over to Cynthia and took a seat across from her. Jabari looked the true Italian woman in her eyes, and he could see the sorrow and stress written all over her face. The scar under her right cheek could easily tell you that she had been through the most, but Jabari's new plan was to rebuild all of that from his own hands. "I know that you don't know me quite well, Mama Cynthia. I've watched this shop for years in this neighborhood, and it means more to me than you think. I'm really here for your daughter, and I would like to keep it that way forever. La familia takes care of each other," Jabari spoke before pulling out the envelope full of cash. Placing it in Cynthia's hand, he held her hand firmly. "I'm here for life," he said before leaning over and placing a kiss on Victoria's cheek.

"Are you okay?" Victoria blinked, trying to figure him out.

"I'm okay. Just watch out for my call. We have to talk," he said before standing up to leave. Nodding his head at Cynthia, he hugged Victoria with so much passion that she could feel the love pouring threw his flesh. He was moving like a brand-new man. She didn't know what he did to send a blessing like thirty thousand dollars her mother's way, but she was grateful for his loyalty and sincerity with making it happen.

"Thank you." She kissed his lips, dreaming that the moment wouldn't end.

Before she could savor the special second, he was gone quicker than the wind. His hat was pulled down low and he was walking out of the bakery, heading back for Keyno's truck. Once he climbed in the passenger's side seat, he huffed, "I'm good."

Keyno stared at him with worry. "Are you positive? You know I'm here if you need more advice."

Jabari looked at the bakery's windows and prayed that the blessing for Cynthia would change a few things for them because his new start was about to make a foundation. "Nah. Let's just get back. Tonight, I'm telling you about the next mission."

Keyno smirked. "Like I said lil bro, whatever you need."

Chapter 15

3 Months Later
C. K McClatchy High School

The graduation was now on the diploma part of the ceremony, and this was the moment Jabari didn't want to present itself. It was time to was across the stage and accept the piece of paper from the same motherfucka that wanted a nigga to work in their burger factory for twenty years and retire an old slave. That damn sure wasn't the future he seen after leaving McClatchy. The diploma wouldn't allow him to see it any different. Hearing the principal call his name to give a school speech, Jabari stood up as the applause rang out loudly. After four years of hard dedication, he managed to keep the highest grade point average, the honor roll list, and credits for a nice college out in Washington if the funds for their family happened to drop on time. Walking past the benches filled with hundreds of teenagers, Jabari stepped in front of the mic and cleared his throat. Cameras were snapping from the crowd. Parents, friends, and family of different graduates sat in the audience waiting for him to give a small testimony about his school life in McClatchy. In his head, he wanted to just tell the average lie the crooked ass law wanted him to, but instead, he decided to keep it realer than real. "I'm literally standing in front of a mic that I feel like I would have never had to get behind in my entire life. It's crazy that I had to work a full twelve years for an acceptance to do more lucrative activities in this world, but hey, what is a dream without having to work hard," he said with a sarcastic tone.

The people sat quietly listening to his story knowing that a good message was coming out of the young brilliant mind.

Jabari gazed out into the crowd and shook his head. "I'm sorry to tell the people of Sacramento this, but this diploma doesn't solidify my spot in this world. It means nothing. I suffered through numerous of years with school just to hear these people tell me I need more education in order to be somebody. Suffering through poverty as a jit, I recognized that really all the valuable rights bestowed upon man were taken at birth. The way that you stamp my name on shit and get money for me through flexing ass accounts, but I guess that's another story.' 'Jabari shrugged in a stupid ass manner. Raising up his high school diploma, he shredded it to pieces.

The crowd gasped, and the reaction from the Mayor of the city wasn't pleasing at all. Jabari snatched the microphone, tapping it lightly. He lowered his tone so he could be heard clearly. "Fuck this diploma saying it made me because I was born a real black one. Wake up," he cursed before walking off.

After the night of Jabari's big lick, he found out that Steven had gotten shipped off to live with his grandparents in Canada after his mother grew sick. She was hospitalized and his best friend slash crew member was knocked down forcing him to work with Blow. Still to that day, he hadn't heard a word, but kept Steven's stash of the money in case he happened to resurface.

Walking past the school's principal, Jabari looked him in the eyes. "Thank you for accepting me, sir, and I thank you for showing me the truth," he whispered before walking through the double doors of their auditorium.

The sun hitting Jabari's face caused him to throw his hand up over his eyes. Snatching the blue cap and gown from his body, he tossed it on the ground and smoothed out his black Gucci collar shirt. His black skinny jeans complimented his white loafers and belt that lightly hung on his hip. Walking across the crowded parking lot of the school, Jabari deactivated the alarm to his new white Dodge Charger SRT. Climbing in the front seat, he huffed before starting the car. It was hard to leave so much behind that he worked for, but the truth was real. The people didn't care about what occurred with you after the graduation. Their only job was to brainwash you with shit that they wanted you to know and send you out into the world. It was hard knock life for a nigga out of Sacramento because if you didn't put in that work, you just wasn't gonna eat.

The sight of Teddy and Leo running across the lot caught his attention. After they both climbed inside, Jabari sparked a blunt and passed it off to Leo.

"Now, can we please get back to business? School is finally over," Teddy asked, leaning over the back seat.

"Hell yeah, Jabari. That lil small ass twenty thou is almost gone. I need some money fast like a lucky foot, and a rabbit's ass," Leo encouraged while pulling on the strawberry Backwoods.

Jabari pulled away from the school before responding. "We still need another driver. I don't trust to many niggas to ride with us on this."

Teddy tapped his shoulder lightly. "Come on Bari, you must have forgotten that we have a whole Nicholas Cage for a little brother. Just use Brandon."

"Hell nah," he quickly dismissed the idea. Ain't no fuckin way his little brother was about to be placed at risk when he was already risking himself on the line to place flood in their mouths.

"He's right though, Jabari. That lil nigga, Brandon, is like the best driver I've ever seen. He's probably the only one close to us who was better than Steven." Leo shook his head before handing the blunt back.

"Man, my little brother is not being placed in this mix. I don't wanna see him hurt. This shit is real, and one slip could be his life."

Teddy smacked his lips. "Mann, nigga look who his big brother is. He got three of us, not including the manic Blow. He has the best position. Sitting in the car where he's safe," Teddy said honestly, before sitting back in the seat.

Jabari grew quiet, evaluating what his brothers was saying. It was very true, but a big brother's love was different with a friend's love. They were moving fast because money was needed, but Jabari was really focused on building and molding Brandon for a different life.

Things grew quiet for a short second before it hit Leo. "Jabari, what about the young dude, Sip, who stay out in Aerojet Road? The one who went to McClatchy for like three months. His mom is the doctor who drives that grey Stingray. The one he used to steal and bust donuts in the school parking lot."

"That young nigga nice too. You talking bout that OSA Gang fast talking lil dude from Atlanta?" Teddy wiggled his hand with a fast nod.

"Yea, the lil hyena looking motherfucker," Leo agreed.

"Who do we suppose to get in contact with him? Do you think we can trust him?" Jabari stopped at the red light, looking over at Leo cautiously.

"Bro, I'm positive. I got his number. If you don't like him after the first move, we can find someone else."

Nodding in silence, Jabari made a left turn, and his eyes met the medium size bank that was next on his list. Now that school was over. He was ready to see what Keyno and Blow truly had to offer. Picking up his phone, he dialed Keyno's number first and received and answer immediately. "Yo, young one. How's the graduation?"

"Wack. I'm ready to work. I'm on my way over," he said before hanging up.

As Leo handled the business with their new driver, Jabari pondered on how shit would be taken over. Within the next few months, he planned on making Sacramento bow to his feet.

City of Kingz

Chapter 16

One Year Later

Jabari's eyes cracked open, and the first thing he spotted was Victoria's beautiful long hair covering half of her face. Her light snoozing could be heard, but she was so gorgeous that he couldn't help but to grin. Leaning over. He placed a kiss on her lips and watched her smile gently. Victoria's eyes fluttered open before she reached out to grab his cheek. "Good morning, handsome."

"Morning, Queen."

Jabari stood up from the bed, and quickly slid his sweatpants over his naked body. Tossing on a Hanes T-shirt, he made his way downstairs. Once Jabari reached the bottom, he grabbed the remote to his seventy-inch plasma and flicked the power button. The new two-story home he purchased was beyond mesmerizing. Six bedrooms, three baths with a banging ass two car garage for his new foreign toys. The decor and furniture inside of his calm walls was dazzling, but also soothing. Money could be smelled every time he stepped out of his house, and the suburban neighborhood he found right outside of Sacramento was a perfect place to build a true relationship with Victoria.

The sound of Keyno's loud ass Hummer motor pulling into his driveway easily faded the television out. You could hear the Nipsey Hussle single, "Rap Niggas" beating behind the dark tinted windows. Jabari smiled once he spotted Strawberry climb from the passenger seat first. Her fire red hair was laying down her shoulders with a light curl at the end. Her skintight Valentino blue jeans matched her light blue Chanel blouse. Her feet was complimented with a thousand-dollar pair of Gucci pumps, and her face could easily make a non-pussy licker suck a bowling ball through a straw. Once Keyno killed the ignition and jumped out, Jabari checked the time on his watch and proceeded towards the door to let his personal inside. It felt good to see Keyno pulling up to his shit. It was sweet for his role model to see him achieve the game at what he did best himself. It wasn't just about the energy to go nuts and raise the guns, but the knowledge to know how you didn't have to always use that shit. It was about the sweet dough. All for the mula and fun.

Opening the front door, Jabari stepped to the side. "Y'all up pretty early I see."

Strawberry pecked his lips and slid right past him. "Yep. It's early and you the only one woke with a full martini bar." She smiled, heading straight for the kitchen.

Jabari laughed at her pushiness and embraced his partner in crime. "Wassup, Keyno? Who's been on her bad side this morning?"

"Come on man. That's Berry. The world is on her bad side." Keyno laughed before stepping inside.

Jabari locked the door and headed towards the living room. "Victoria is asleep. You guys actually caught me at the perfect time." He flopped down on the couch and looked over at Strawberry with a grin. She had that ass tooted up on his barstool like she didn't wanna to bothered.

Keyno decided to stand and place his attention on the TV. The world news was speaking about high crime rates, and violence throughout the state of California. He knew that Jabari wanted to stay in tune with everything when it came down to his new profession. The time frame. The movements. Every large to small coordination. Keyno respected his mind, and that was enough to let him lead the pack. "So wassup, young one? I've been thinking on a money train and I'm trying to see where we at with this new gig?" Keyno asked curiously.

Jabari nodded quietly as if he was contemplating it all in his head before he answered. "We're close enough. I was swerving around the upper city yesterday trying to make sure it all was official. The alarm system is rooted to the money boxes, and if the drawer is opened incorrectly, it's gonna trigger a silent call out to the four closest police precincts. This is gonna take all of us. The safe is probably holding about 2.5 mil tops. If we split even from that and the counter money, we all looking at four-hundred and seventy-five thousand a piece. We all agree to cut Strawberry a hundred grand for her role, and the extras will be for Sip and the getaway crews."

Keyno smiled gratefully. "When did you figure all this juicy ass stuff out?"

"Like I said, I've been doing my homework. I say we got a cool four days to rest before we make this shit happen. If we slay this job, I think that'll actually put me at the number one spot on the United States public enemy list." Jabari laughed before stretching his arms.

"Good." Keyno clasped his hands in excitement. His face would always glow up when Jabari laid down the foundation of how the mission was about to take place. It cut all chances of any lacking to interfere. He was the new mastermind of the business, and shit didn't operate accordingly when the position was in the hands of a fool. Jabari was that assurance to make sure that word was kept far away from their vocabularies.

"So, what's gonna take place after this? Sacramento is starting to bite my ass and we're gonna need a whole new location if we ain't trying to end up going on a double date with the Feds." Strawberry sipped the last of her beverage seductively.

"The Feds don't like me." Jabari smirked. "I've been on the move for a year, and I think that they've finally gotten a small glimpse of my shoes on the news. I love this shit. It's like hide and seek. We started off taking little jobs, and now we moving on to our eighth bank. I've been counting down, and now I think we need to spread out a bit."

Keyno sparked his cotton candy Kush and nearly chocked. "What the hell you mean spread out?"

"Be easy old man. Not too far away, and it won't be for long. I was thinking maybe we go and pull a few jobs out in San Diego. The bigger the better, and it'll also give us time to let the city power down a while. This shit is inferno hot, and we maybe have one more bank before the National Guards start patrolling the streets of Sacramento. Seriously, we need a break," Jabari suggested before fixing his own shot of Remy V. S. O. P.

"If that's what you feel needs to be done, I'm pushing right behind ya, Bari. The call is on you."

Brandon slowly made his way down the staircase with a huge smile when he heard Keyno agree to his brother's request. "So, let me get this right. Are we finally making out this bitch?" His eyes roamed between all of them to see if he could receive a positive answer.

Jabari shrugged with a smile. "Pack you a bag in a few weeks, Champ. We got money to make out in San Diego."

"Shittt nigga, you ain't got to tell me twice." He rubbed his hands, heading back up the stairs.

Strawberry looked over at Jabari with an inquisitive expression. "Does he know?"

"No, he doesn't, but I don't wanna put so much pressure on him. That's why I'm gonna keep it a surprise until we get there. I was kind of hoping that this would cheer him up. Robbing banks isn't the path I paved for my little brother, but I know how the feeling could make somebody get. I'm trying to keep some type of sanity in his head before he turns into Robert DeNiro from the movie *Heat*."

Keyno laughed, but knew Jabari was beyond serious. Brandon was the new addition to their team, and so far, he was the best getaway driver the police force ever witnessed to step on a gas pedal. It was a bad reputation to be so deep in the game, but a damn good hustle to be so young with a quarter million stashed just from driving.

"Well, we love you both. Just make sure you're not rushing into this too fast. I know how it feels to not have my mama. I haven't seen my old lady since I was seven, so Brandon is probably gonna react a little different. Good luck, young one. I'ma give you a call later and see how it went." Keyno shook hands with Jabari and headed for the front door.

Strawberry followed suite by giving him a firm hug and whispered delicately into his ear, "Just because you're engaged doesn't mean you ain't gotta handle your business, Jabari. Don't be getting brand new." She clawed her nails lightly into his back with an upset face.

"In due time, Strawberry." He placed a light kiss on her forehead and watched as she walked out behind Keyno.

Jabari chuckled lightly. A woman who laid down a territory stamp on a young one was surely bound to feel agitated around another's Queen's throne. Still in all, Strawberry showed major respect and always held those feelings beneath her thick red skin.

Brandon snapped him out of the lovebird trance when he appeared back downstairs. "Why the hell you standing around looking like you just missed the last episode of *Snowfall?*"

"Nah, I'm good, Champ. I need you to ride somewhere with me though."

Brandon nodded with a curious face. "Cool, but where the hell are we going this early? I was about to head out with Blow and Sip in a few. They wanted to take me shopping."

"Not today. We got other things to handle. I want you to spend a little time with your big brother. Plus, I need you with me when I pull up on some close family. I just wanna try and slide away from the team for a second, ya know," Jabari offered. He didn't want to give up the news about him finding the whereabouts of their mother just yet. He also knew that it was a hard mission to force his younger brother back into their past that was left behind them so many years ago.

"Whatever you say, Jabari. When are we leaving?" Brandon asked, moving towards the kitchen table for a glass of orange juice.

"Probably in a few. I'm gonna make a call to ensure that we will arrive at the right time. I'm about to grab a shower real quick and we out of here," Jabari informed him before walking off.

It was hard being captured in the bounds of Sacramento with the background of making yourself a self-sufficient man. A man that had to care for a fifteen-year-old brother as if he was already grown at the age of a teen. Jabari knew that times were hard on most people who came up from Hagginwood, but that statement wouldn't remain the same legacy for him and his little champ. He was proud to say that he actually did it without a mother or father. That alone made him believe that being a King of your city was destined for only the strong believers. Now, it was time to show everyone else that he could sit the State of California on his back and do the same.

City of Kingz

Chapter 17

Small Regional-Mental Institution
Sacramento, California

Pulling in front of large medical building, Jabari slid his new silver 2018 Range Rover smoothly through the lot, parked, and shut off his engine. Looking over at Brandon, he smiled. "We're here, bro."

"A hospital? You stopped me from a day of shopping with the guys to bring me to a hospital, Jabari?" he asked with a screwed-up face.

"Patience little grasshopper. You don't even know our purpose for being here. This might be the only chance to get a few answers that you wanted. It's not a vain trip, but you have to trust me."

Brandon huffed, but agreed by opening his car door to step out. Jabari knew that the sight of their mother could possibly go the opposite way that he planned, but that was a chance he was willing take in order to see things clear up his little brother's questions about their past history.

As the boys made their way to the entrance, Jabari stepped inside first and made his way to the front desk. An elderly white man occupied the area, and his hands were busy tapping away at the laptop that rested in front of him when Jabari cleared his throat. "Excuse me, sir. My name is Mr. Salters. I'm the one who contacted you about the visit yesterday."

"Oh yes indeed. Jabari, correct?" The doctor wiggled his finger as if he had to take a wild guess.

"Yes sir."

"I've been waiting for you two. You're about twenty minutes late, but it's no biggie. Follow me if you will."

The doctor jumped to his feet and began to trail down a long hallway that rested directly across from him.

Jabari and Brandon remained quiet as they walked closely behind him. The small trip stopped when the doctor opened a set of double doors. The large room behind it was big enough to host a small event. It would remind you of a nursing home if it didn't have the large windows around the area allowing you to see the beautiful city view. There were flat screen televisions mounted in three different areas and there was at least twelve visiting tables available for use.

When Jabari's eyes landed on their mother sitting with her back turned, his heart shuffled. He quickly looked at the doctor and placed two crispy hundred-dollar bills into his palm. "Thank you so much, Doc. I'll take it from here."

"Sure thing Mr. Salters. You guys have thirty minutes, and I'll be returning." He nodded humbly and walked back through the double doors.

Brandon covered his nose in a joking manner. "This shit smells like a doo-doo factory. This isn't the average fun for a teenager, Jabari. I hope you didn't volunteer me to do anything with nobody here," he mumbled, looking around.

"Yes, I volunteered you to meet her," he replied, pointing over to their mother.

"Who is she?" Brandon asked with a confused expression while staring at the grey-haired woman. A black beauty mark rested under her eye and her wrinkled skin would give you the impression that she was easily over the age of sixty. "Who is she?"

Jabari walked closer with Brandon until they stood face to face with the woman who gave birth to them both. "Little bro, I would like you to meet our mother, Crystal

Salters. Hello mom," Jabari said forcing her to look up from the crossword puzzle she was occupied with.

Crystal slowly raised her eyes and smiled from ear to ear. "Jabari and Benson. Oh, my God. My babies!" She covered her mouth in shock.

"His name is Brandon, mama," Jabari corrected before leaning over to give her a hug.

"Oh goodness, that's right. Brandon. It's all the same thing to me, boy. Come over here and give your mama a hug, Benson," Crystal said, getting his name incorrect again.

Brandon's face was lost for words. Throughout his life of growing up, he never envisioned meeting his mother at the age of fifteen. And now that she was finally in front of him, she couldn't even get his name right. He could definitely tell that the stories about her being on drugs was surely the reason for her psychotic meltdown, especially judging from the thick black bags under her eyes. Brandon was about to deny her request for a hug until he caught Jabari ice grilling him as if he was daring him to buck. Leaning down to embrace Crystal in a quick hug, he quickly released her and folded his arms.

"How are my babies? Are y'all coming to stay with mama for a little while?" Crystal said looking back and forth between them both.

"We came to visit, mama. We haven't seen you in a very long time. Brandon hasn't seen you since he was born. It's been almost fifteen years, mama," Jabari said with a straight face.

"It hasn't been that long, Jabari. Y'all just came and seen me a few months ago. Now stop overexaggerating before I put yo ass on punishment. You know I don't like liars," she said, searching for another word on her puzzle.

"I'm out of here," Brandon whispered to Jabari through clenched teeth. "This lady doesn't even know who the hell we are."

"You're not going anywhere. Show some respect and remember that this is our mother. She's sick, little bro. What the fuck do you expect? You don't care about meeting the woman who birthed you, huh?" Jabari eyes widened, waiting for an answer.

Instead of replying, Brandon remained quiet with his chest heaving lightly. It hurt to see the woman who claimed to be their mama get her own son's name wrong after being missing in action for so long. It was pointless to come around if she wasn't in the right condition to know who was standing in front of her.

Jabari turned back to his mother and placed a hand on her small fragile arm. "Mama, is there anything you wanna know about us? We've been waiting to see you. I'm sure you have some questions for your boys because we surely missed you," he asked, trying to build a conversation. Brandon stood behind him quietly with a blank expression.

"Yes baby. Where is your brother, Kentavious?" she asked with seriousness lacing her tone.

The name caused Jabari to screw up his face. "Mama, you don't have a son named Kentavious. It's just me and Brandon. Your two boys. Remember?"

Crystal pointed a stern finger towards him as if she was fed up with his deceit. Her lips started to tremble with anger, and Jabari stood up straight just in case she spazzed out or tried to strike him. "Motherfucker, I'll slap the hell out of you. I know how many kids came out my pussy, little boy. You, Benson, and your older brother, Kentavious. Now where the hell is he?"

Brandon chuckled to himself before throwing his hands in the air. "In order to get her straight, we will definitely have to find Benson and Kentavious because I think we got the wrong lady. Can we leave?"

Jabari's mouth twisted in anger at his little brother's disrespectful statement. "Chill, little nigga."

"Nah, you chill motherfucker. Don't talk to Benson like that. Get yo ass out of my house, boy," Crystal shouted towards Jabari as if he was the one acting belligerent. "You think I'm crazy nigga! If you not stepping in here with my baby Kentavious, then I don't want you here either," she snapped before placing her attention back on the crossword puzzle in her hand.

Jabari's heart literally quaked with pain from the way his mother's words spilled from her lips. After years of thinking that she may have healed from the terrible illness, it was finally clear that her days of being a parent to them once again would possibly never happen.

Doctor Fitzgerald moved swiftly back through the double doors after hearing Crystal's voice rise. Not trying to take the chance of her having a panic attack, he placed his hand on Jabari's shoulder. "Maybe that's enough for today, Mr. Salters. It's probably best if you try at another time," he suggested before passing Crystal a small cup of water with her morning medication.

"I'm not taking shit, Mr. Fitzberry. Where is Kentavious? You lied and said he was coming. You is a bitch ass doctor for that shit," Crystal spat as he helped her up from the chair.

Jabari shook his head in disbelief before cutting his eyes over to Brandon. His little brother's attitude was definitely showing, and it was clear that he didn't expect to see or hear the things that just occurred with the woman who claimed to be his biological mother. It made it even harder to understand when that same woman couldn't even pronounce his name correctly.

Instead of asking if he was okay, Jabari placed a hand on his shoulder. "I'm sorry. Let's just go," he mumbled before heading towards the exit.

The thought of just having a small piece of family was going down the drain daily. Their mother was drifting away, their father was deceased, and all they had now was each other. After going through the painful motions for so long, Jabari was actually ready to accept the fact that Brandon was all he had, and by any means necessary, he would make sure his little champ never wanted for anything ever again.

Chapter 18

Two Days Later
River's City Bank & Loans

The sun was just beginning to rise at its highest peak when Jabari spotted the manager of the facility finally opening the front door for the waiting bankers. Keyno was sure to keep his eyes focused on the two intersecting streets before he gave the call for the team to move in. The large bank held over five tellers, two security guards, and eight cameras that was bound to catch a glimpse of your identity if you didn't wear the proper facemask. Numerous of attempts was made against the high-profile cash house and it was roughly sixteen years ago since their last successful robbery. The last crew who attempted failed horribly by losing three men from a few bullets and one man who was currently spending the rest of his natural life in a super max prison that was located in the center of Colorado. The Sacramento Police Force was sure to place extra protection on the facility because of the large amounts of cash that was held inside. So, getting in and out was surely about to be the fella's biggest task. The one thing Jabari was sure of was his capability to handle the job, or at least die trying. No matter how tough that shit seemed, he was determined that he was walking back out that door with every coin. One of the small walkie radio's sounding off broke his small trance.

"Keyno, what the hell are we waiting for? This is the time to move in before traffic begins to pour out on the main street," Blow spoke through the device. He was already in place, waiting in the passenger of Sip's getaway car and his urge to grab that dough was pumping harder than a two-inch dick on a horny sixty-year-old man.

"I know what I'm doing, Blow. Just have patience. We only got a minute or so left. Stay off the radio, we don't need Leo's radio scanner picking up anything from the precinct. Stay off the radio," he ordered before looking over to Jabari. "Whenever you say go, lil bro, we're moving. It's your call."

Jabari remained quiet. Teddy and Leo sat with their heads lowered, guns in hand. They were prepared to handle the business and talking about it was the last thing on either of their minds. As seconds clicked by on his time piece, Jabari watched as one of the customers exited the bank, and made the call, "Go!"

Wasting no time, the four of them jumped out of the vehicle moving quickly across the large parking lot. The sight of Blow leaping out of Sip's car with two men behind him matched perfectly with the rhythm of the team. Their large assault rifles were held out in front of them and they all reached the front door at the same time. Jabari led the way through the entrance and grabbed the first guard's attention immediately. Using the handle of his M-16 assault rifle, he slammed it roughly into his stomach.

"Get the fuck down and don't move, bitch!" he growled with spittle flying from his mouth.

Blow moved forward with his two workers directly behind him, aiming his gun at the ceiling. He released two shots.

Boom! Boom!

"If you don't wanna know what a fucking hollow tip bullet feels like, I would suggest y'all bitches get down on the floor and freeze ya self like a piece of cold pussy!"

The citizens wasted no time dropping down as if they were all doused with a shot of the coronavirus. Leo and Teddy aimed their guns towards the bank tellers and jumped across the counters within seconds. "Back up, back up. Hands on top of your head!" Teddy screamed, pushing them one by one towards the wall.

It didn't take long for the fellas to get the entire building under control, and once the noise ceased, Jabari clicked the timer on his watch for two minutes. Moving over to the bank manager's desk, he tapped him lightly with his foot. "Hey, you. I'm not sure if you know what the fuck is going on, but this is a robbery dumbass. Get up and come bust this fucking vault open! And don't make me say it twice."

The man shook uncontrollably with his hands held high in the air. "Sir-rr p-please. I'll give you whatever you need. Just don't shoot." The man fumbled with his hands in fear.

Jabari's eyes grew wider. "Move!"

Jumping into action, the bank manager walked over to the large steel gate and entered a seven-digit code. The compressed vault released a small amount of air allowing the door to swing open with ease. Pushing the scary man against the floor, Jabari stepped inside and released his tension after locking eyes on the neatly stacked cash. It was definitely more than enough to carry, and a payday wasn't the word with all the bills that sat stored inside of the four thick walls.

Tossing the bags from his back on the floor, he waved the gun towards the manager. "Fill 'em up. Now!"

Without wasting time, the man rushed towards the cash and began to push the paper inside of the bag at a fast pace.

Jabari checked his time piece while keeping his eyes on Teddy and Leo who cleared the bank cabinets with ease.

Blow continued to circle the floor with his two masked goons standing guard at the front door. "We got one minute!" he yelled before placing his attention back on the manager.

After the two bags was filled, Jabari tossed them both around his shoulder and aimed his gun back at the man's head. "Get back out to the big floor. Let's go!"

Doing what he was told, the manager held his hands high and walked out of the vault. Jabari kicked him in the back watching him fall to the floor. "We only got a few seconds left, guys. Tighten up so we can move out."

Keyno grabbed one of the bags from Leo and quickly tossed it across his back. His eyes continued to look at citizens who aligned the floor, and the that's when it happened.

"Stop moving motherfucker! Blow yelled before releasing a bullet into a man's head, killing him instantly.

Boc!

The loud bang caused a few civilians to scream and cover their heads in fear. Keyno turned to face Blow and spotted one of the hostages reaching for a handgun on his hip. Blow was yelling so loud that he never noticed the man about to take his life. Raising his gun, Keyno fired his weapon twice, knocking a chunk out of the man's cranium.

Boom! Boom!

"What the fuck just happened? Why did you shoot?" Jabari moved over to Blow and pushed him recklessly.

"Fuck that nigga. He was reaching," he fired back.

"Guys, we have to go now. Our time is up!" Teddy yelled, breaking towards the front door with a huge bag on his back.

Jabari bit his tongue for the second, but the sloppy ass mistake was damn sure gonna be addressed when they made it away from the scene. "Let's go!" he said, running directly behind Teddy out of the front door.

Keyno was sure to keep his gun aimed on the remaining citizens to ensure everyone made it out safe. After Leo brushed pass him out of the front door, he watched as Blow reached down for the dead officer's gold Rolex watch. "Nigga, let's go. Fuck that shit. We didn't come for that shit, bro."

Snatching the jewelry, he rushed for the door, and nearly fell trying to pass by Keyno. Once the sun pierced both of their skins, the sound of the loud police sirens could be heard as they began to pour out of the intersecting streets behind them. Blow wasted no time firing six shots to let them know that going to prison wasn't an option.

Boc! Boc! Boc! Boc! Boc! Boc!

They both could see Jabari and Sip's car posted on the opposite side of the street, but the Sacramento Police Department was beginning to spill from everywhere. Car tires were screeching, and traffic was starting to slide over to the side of the road when Blow took his chances and sprinted across the street in front of the flying vehicles. Before Keyno could dash behind him. A barrel of shots began to rang out loudly. The bullet that pierced his leg forced him cringe and crumble to the ground.

Jabari was standing at the driver's side of his whip when he watched his close friend hit the ground. Aiming his weapon at the group of police officers, he let off ten rapid shots forcing them to take cover behind their vehicles.

Pak! Pak! Pak! Pak! Pak! Pak! Pak!

The semi-automatic burped loudly.

"Keyno, get up. You gotta get up!" Jabari cried out.

"We have to go, Jabari!" Leo screamed, cranking up the engine.

Keyno struggled to stand from the gunshot wound, but he managed to climb back to his feet. "Just go little bro!" he shouted realizing that the car was too far for him to make it.

Jabari continued to pop his gun at the cops forcing their heads to retreat back behind their cruisers. Blow's driver, Sip, smashed off with him, leaving them alone to fend against the authorities of the law. "Keyno, get up!"

Struggling to absorb with the horrible pain in his leg, he tried to move again. The time seemed to freeze in slow motion when one of the officer's raised up with his twelve-gauge shotgun, pulling the trigger. The large slug slammed into Keyno's back sending a chunk flying from his stomach.

Booom!

"Nooooo!" Jabari screamed as he watched his friend's face cave into the concrete.

Leo witnessed the tragedy but refused to let his brother go out bad. Snatching him by the arm, he pulled him towards the Impala and shoved him in. "Go Teddy! Go!" he screamed as the bullets began to ricochet off of their getaway vehicle. Ducking from the shattering glass of the back window, Teddy mashed his foot on the gas, forcefully speeding away from the scene.

Chapter 19

Jabari's House
Twenty Minutes Later

As Teddy swerved the car inside of Jabari's yard, they all grabbed the large bags of cash and headed inside. Sip's car was parked on the side of the house, alerting him that Blow had already arrived minutes before them. Rushing through the front door, Jabari's eyes landed on Blow sitting next to his two workers and Strawberry inside of living room. Dropping the bag, he ran straight towards him, landing a hard-right fist across his jaw and sending him to the floor. "Why did you shoot? You fucked up everything. Why did you fucking shoot, idiot?" Jabari yelled, striking him again.

"That motherfucker was reaching, nigga. He had a gun!" Blow forced himself to swing back, but the crew separated them before another lick could be thrown.

Leo stepped in between the two with a sad expression. "Everybody needs to chill the fuck out, man! If we do this right now, were all bound to be in jail by end of the night. We need to take a deep breath and talk like we got some common sense. This conversation isn't for the whole neighborhood," he said, looking back and forth between the both of them.

Jabari released his negative energy by taking a deep breath. He began to rub his temples and took a seat on the couch. Strawberry walked over to him and eased down by his side. "Jabari, where is Keyno?"

He could tell by the tone of her voice that she already knew the answer. It was never promised for shit to go perfect in the line of business the team was involved with, but slip ups was something she knew Jabari and Keyno didn't accept. His silence said everything she needed to know, and Strawberry's eyes slightly teared up when he shook his head in defeat.

Standing to his feet, he moved over to his Samsung flat screen television, turned it straight to the Channel 5 News. The white reporter's voice boomed through the speakers, causing Strawberry and the crew to gather around.

"This is news reporter, Sam Crotters, and we are here today at the Rivers City Bank on 925 L Street. Apparently, a robbery has taken place at this government facility leaving one undercover officer and a civilian dead. This bank is one of the most secured in the city of Sacramento and hasn't been in harm's way in over sixteen years according to the records. Investigators are questioning witnesses who were present during the crime and currently checking surveillance cameras inside to see exactly who committed this horrendous act. Word from the authorities says that the job was obviously tackled by a group of professionals. Over three-million dollars was stolen from the building. And after questioning a few civilians who were being held hostage, the police force began to check all surveillance cameras around the area. We are suspecting it to be about five to six suspects on the loose, and one of the armed robbers was murdered on the scene by Detective Pakori of the Sacramento Police Department. That's all the information we have on this case right now, and authorities have asked if anybody finds out any information to please contact the police hotline. Back to you, Susie," the reporter informed.

Ripping the flat screen from the wall, Jabari slung it across his living room with ease, startling everyone before walking out on his back porch.

Leo cut his eyes over to Strawberry. "Can you please calm him down? You're probably the only one who can at this moment."

She knew that he was right and losing the leader of their crew was something they couldn't help but to accept at the moment. Jabari was next in line to keep shit in order, so watching him lose himself was out of the question. Nodding at Leo, she headed towards the back patio door and stepped out. Jabari posted against the railing of his balcony, staring into the sky. There was no way to actually tell him that he was wrong about how he felt, but it was also no turning back when the crew began to involve themselves into a life of crime and taking money from banks. It was the roots of evil that came with the hand they dealt, and sometimes, the hand you got could deal you right out of the game. Wrapping her hands around his waist, she hugged him tightly before releasing a few tears.

"I know that I can't bring your friend back to you. I know this. I also know that we need you to remain strong for the ones who can't fill Keyno's shoes, Jabari. You are the smartest young man that I know when it comes down too handling your business. If you break right now, this team will disintegrate. I know that you haven't known me forever, but this small time has given me tons of motivation from you. Please don't let it stop now," she said before kissing his cheek, and leaving him to himself.

Evaluating Strawberry's strong words, he knew that she was damn sure right. Keyno's face ran through his mind and it would be hard to continue without the one who gave him the same motivation he enforced on everyone else. Wiping the light tear that cascaded down his face, he promised himself to keep Keyno's words close to his heart.

Following his steps would always ensure Jabari to win, and that was a key he'd go by forever.

"City of Kingz, my nigga. I love you forever," he mumbled to himself before kissing Keyno's dog tags that rested on his neck.

Chapter 20

One Week Later

The loud banging on Jabari's front door caused him to roll over quickly out of his sleep and grab his Ruger P89 pistol. Cynthia was sitting up in the bed with a nervous face. Her hands were shaking profusely as if she knew who was causing the disturbing noise. Placing a finger to his lip, he gestured for her to be quiet and jumped swiftly to his feet.

Walking out into his hallway, he held the gun out in front of him and moved downstairs. Brandon, Blow, and Teddy was stretched out on the floor. Judging from the liquor bottles laying near them, they wouldn't be able to hear if Santa Claus came skimming down the fucking chimney. The loud knocking started again causing Jabari to move towards the door. Stepping over Teddy, he kicked his foot and forced him to wake up.

"What? Who is it?" He jumped up and grabbed his gun from underneath the living room table.

Shushing him, Jabari got to the door and placed his eye up to the peephole. Realizing that it was Leo, he exhaled with relief and opened the door.

"Nigga, why the hell you acting like you got a warrant to come in this motherfucker? You know it's a bunch of bank robbers in this bitch, right?" Jabari walked off, allowing him to enter.

"Yeah, yeah. Fuck all that. All y'all niggas get the fuck up. We need to talk. Yo Brandon, Blow, get the fuck up," he said, looking at his drunk ass brothers sprawled out on the floor.

"Mannnn, if you ain't got no pussy with you, stop yelling and get the fuck out dork ass nigga. We been up all night already." Blow yawned, rolling out of his sleep.

Brandon stretched his arms and stood to his feet, following Jabari and Leo into the kitchen. After all of the fellas gathered at the kitchen table, Leo turned his attention to Jabari who was pouring a fresh cup of OJ. "Now that all of y'all are woke, I have a question. What is more important than money?" Leo asked looking at all of them.

Brandon chuckled before nudging Blow. "Pussy wrapped in a hundred-dollar bill."

Even Jabari couldn't help but to laugh from his little brother's stupid remark.

Leo shook his head, pacing back and forth. "That was cute, but no. I'm talking about more money. That's what's better."

"And what's your point, Dexter Laboratory?" Teddy yawned, trying to cut the small talk.

Leo pulled a large light blue piece of paper from his pocket and unfolded it, placing it on the table. The crew gathered around and stared down at the shit he claimed was so important.

Blow was the first to make a stupid comment, "What is this, build a bank instructions? We're robbers, lil nigga, not architects."

"For your info, it's not a bank, ass," Leo corrected him humbly.

Jabari's eyes scanned the paper curiously. "So, what's the catch?"

"It's no catch. It's our next lick," he replied.

"What bank is this cause it only looks like the outline of that motherfucka?" Teddy asked.

"It's not a bank, genius," Leo huffed.

"What is it?" Jabari questioned.

Forming a devilish smile, Leo leaned down. "It's a casino."

"What, a casino? Who the hell you think we are, nigga, Robert DeNiro? This ain't *Ocean's Twelve*. Leo, that's kinda out of our league, don't ya think?" Teddy cocked his neck to the side.

"Where is it located?" Jabari asked, ignoring Teddy's weak ass faith.

"Las Vegas. I'm doing my homework on everything now. Veronica gave me the layout of her dad's establishment and she blessed us with the blueprints. We've made it to the major leagues, baby." Leo smiled.

"I'm down with that shit sho'nuff." Blow grinned from ear to ear.

"Hell the fuck yeah. Me too," Brandon repeated behind him.

"Everybody calm down," Jabari said, looking over at Leo. "How much money you talking here?"

"Fifteen to twenty million dollars max," he confirmed.

Just from the sound of the large number caused Jabari's hands to sweat in anticipation. Shit was officially real, and it was damn sure on another level from the average ass banks they were used to taking down. Still in all, scared money didn't make no money. Keyno would be smiling harder than a kid with a bucket of candy if he was there to hear the status of Leo's new caper.

Jabari rubbed a finger across his chin before looking up at Leo. "Do you think it's possible?"

"That's like asking me if you are the smartest nigga I know."

Forcing a smile, he nodded. "Get the crew prepared and find some faster cars. We're heading to Vegas, fellas," Jabari confirmed before sparking his blunt.

To Be Continued...
City of Kingz 2
Coming Soon

Submission Guideline

Submit the first three chapters of your completed manuscript to ldpsubmissions@gmail.com, subject line: Your book's title. The manuscript must be in a .doc file and sent as an attachment. Document should be in Times New Roman, double spaced and in size 12 font. Also, provide your synopsis and full contact information. If sending multiple submissions, they must each be in a separate email.

Have a story but no way to send it electronically? You can still submit to LDP/Ca$h Presents. Send in the first three chapters, written or typed, of your completed manuscript to:

LDP: Submissions Dept
Po Box 944
Stockbridge, Ga 30281

DO NOT send original manuscript. Must be a duplicate.

Provide your synopsis and a cover letter containing your full contact information.

Thanks for considering LDP and Ca$h Presents.

Coming Soon from Lock Down Publications/Ca$h Presents

BOW DOWN TO MY GANGSTA

By **Ca$h**

TORN BETWEEN TWO

By **Coffee**

THE STREETS STAINED MY SOUL **II**

By **Marcellus Allen**

BLOOD OF A BOSS **VI**

SHADOWS OF THE GAME II

By **Askari**

LOYAL TO THE GAME **IV**

By **T.J. & Jelissa**

A DOPEBOY'S PRAYER **II**

By **Eddie "Wolf" Lee**

IF LOVING YOU IS WRONG... **III**

By **Jelissa**

TRUE SAVAGE **VII**

MIDNIGHT CARTEL III

DOPE BOY MAGIC IV

CITY OF KINGZ II

By **Chris Green**

BLAST FOR ME **III**

A SAVAGE DOPEBOY III

CUTTHROAT MAFIA II

By **Ghost**

A HUSTLER'S DECEIT III

Chris Green

KILL ZONE **II**
BAE BELONGS TO ME III
A DOPE BOY'S QUEEN II
By **Aryanna**
COKE KINGS V
KING OF THE TRAP II
By **T.J. Edwards**
GORILLAZ IN THE BAY V
De'Kari
THE STREETS ARE CALLING II
Duquie Wilson
KINGPIN KILLAZ IV
STREET KINGS III
PAID IN BLOOD III
CARTEL KILLAZ IV
DOPE GODS II
Hood Rich
SINS OF A HUSTLA II
ASAD
KINGZ OF THE GAME V
Playa Ray
SLAUGHTER GANG IV
RUTHLESS HEART IV
By Willie Slaughter
THE HEART OF A SAVAGE III
By Jibril Williams
FUK SHYT II

180

City of Kingz

By Blakk Diamond

FEAR MY GANGSTA 5

THE REALEST KILLAS

By Tranay Adams

TRAP GOD II

By Troublesome

YAYO IV

A SHOOTER'S AMBITION III

By S. Allen

GHOST MOB

Stilloan Robinson

KINGPIN DREAMS III

By Paper Boi Rari

CREAM

By Yolanda Moore

SON OF A DOPE FIEND II

By Renta

FOREVER GANGSTA II

GLOCKS ON SATIN SHEETS III

By Adrian Dulan

LOYALTY AIN'T PROMISED II

By Keith Williams

THE PRICE YOU PAY FOR LOVE II

DOPE GIRL MAGIC III

By Destiny Skai

CONFESSIONS OF A GANGSTA II

By Nicholas Lock

I'M NOTHING WITHOUT HIS LOVE II

By Monet Dragun

CAUGHT UP IN THE LIFE III

By Robert Baptiste

LIFE OF A SAVAGE IV

A GANGSTA'S QUR'AN II

By **Romell Tukes**

QUIET MONEY III

THUG LIFE II

By **Trai'Quan**

THE STREETS MADE ME III

By **Larry D. Wright**

THE ULTIMATE SACRIFICE VI

IF YOU CROSSM ME ONCE II

By **Anthony Fields**

THE LIFE OF A HOOD STAR

By Ca$h & Rashia Wilson

Available Now

RESTRAINING ORDER **I & II**

By **CA$H & Coffee**

LOVE KNOWS NO BOUNDARIES **I II & III**

By **Coffee**

RAISED AS A GOON I, II, III & IV

BRED BY THE SLUMS I, II, III

BLAST FOR ME I & II

ROTTEN TO THE CORE I II III

A BRONX TALE I, II, III

DUFFEL BAG CARTEL I II III IV

HEARTLESS GOON I II III IV

A SAVAGE DOPEBOY I II

HEARTLESS GOON I II III

DRUG LORDS I II III

CUTTHROAT MAFIA

By **Ghost**

LAY IT DOWN **I & II**

LAST OF A DYING BREED

BLOOD STAINS OF A SHOTTA I & II III

By **Jamaica**

LOYAL TO THE GAME I II III

LIFE OF SIN I, II III

By **TJ & Jelissa**

BLOODY COMMAS I & II

SKI MASK CARTEL I II & III

KING OF NEW YORK I II,III IV V

RISE TO POWER I II III

COKE KINGS I II III IV

BORN HEARTLESS I II III IV

KING OF THE TRAP

By **T.J. Edwards**

Chris Green

IF LOVING HIM IS WRONG…I & II
LOVE ME EVEN WHEN IT HURTS I II III
By **Jelissa**
WHEN THE STREETS CLAP BACK I & II III
THE HEART OF A SAVAGE I II
By **Jibril Williams**
A DISTINGUISHED THUG STOLE MY HEART I II & III
LOVE SHOULDN'T HURT I II III IV
RENEGADE BOYS I II III IV
PAID IN KARMA I II III
By **Meesha**
A GANGSTER'S CODE I &, II III
A GANGSTER'S SYN I II III
THE SAVAGE LIFE I II III
CHAINED TO THE STREETS I II III
By J-Blunt
PUSH IT TO THE LIMIT
By **Bre' Hayes**
BLOOD OF A BOSS **I, II, III, IV, V**
SHADOWS OF THE GAME
By **Askari**
THE STREETS BLEED MURDER **I, II & III**
THE HEART OF A GANGSTA I II& III
By **Jerry Jackson**
CUM FOR ME I II III IV V
An **LDP Erotica Collaboration**
BRIDE OF A HUSTLA **I II & II**

184

THE FETTI GIRLS **I, II& III**

CORRUPTED BY A GANGSTA I, II III, IV

BLINDED BY HIS LOVE

THE PRICE YOU PAY FOR LOVE

DOPE GIRL MAGIC I II

By **Destiny Skai**

WHEN A GOOD GIRL GOES BAD

By **Adrienne**

THE COST OF LOYALTY I II III

By Kweli

A GANGSTER'S REVENGE **I II III & IV**

THE BOSS MAN'S DAUGHTERS I II III IV V

A SAVAGE LOVE **I & II**

BAE BELONGS TO ME I II

A HUSTLER'S DECEIT I, II, III

WHAT BAD BITCHES DO I, II, III

SOUL OF A MONSTER I II III

KILL ZONE

A DOPE BOY'S QUEEN

By **Aryanna**

A KINGPIN'S AMBITON

A KINGPIN'S AMBITION **II**

I MURDER FOR THE DOUGH

By **Ambitious**

TRUE SAVAGE I II III IV V VI

DOPE BOY MAGIC I, II, III

MIDNIGHT CARTEL I II

CITY OF KINGZ

By **Chris Green**

A DOPEBOY'S PRAYER

By **Eddie "Wolf" Lee**

THE KING CARTEL **I, II & III**

By **Frank Gresham**

THESE NIGGAS AIN'T LOYAL **I, II & III**

By **Nikki Tee**

GANGSTA SHYT **I II &III**

By **CATO**

THE ULTIMATE BETRAYAL

By **Phoenix**

BOSS'N UP **I , II & III**

By **Royal Nicole**

I LOVE YOU TO DEATH

By Destiny J

I RIDE FOR MY HITTA

I STILL RIDE FOR MY HITTA

By **Misty Holt**

LOVE & CHASIN' PAPER

By **Qay Crockett**

TO DIE IN VAIN

SINS OF A HUSTLA

By **ASAD**

BROOKLYN HUSTLAZ

By **Boogsy Morina**

BROOKLYN ON LOCK I & II

City of Kingz

By **Sonovia**
GANGSTA CITY
By **Teddy Duke**
A DRUG KING AND HIS DIAMOND I & II III
A DOPEMAN'S RICHES
HER MAN, MINE'S TOO I, II
CASH MONEY HO'S
By Nicole Goosby
TRAPHOUSE KING **I II & III**
KINGPIN KILLAZ I II III
STREET KINGS I II
PAID IN BLOOD **I II**
CARTEL KILLAZ I II III
DOPE GODS
By **Hood Rich**
LIPSTICK KILLAH **I, II, III**
CRIME OF PASSION I II & III
By **Mimi**
STEADY MOBBN' **I, II, III**
THE STREETS STAINED MY SOUL
By **Marcellus Allen**
WHO SHOT YA **I, II, III**
SON OF A DOPE FIEND
Renta
GORILLAZ IN THE BAY **I II III IV**
TEARS OF A GANGSTA I II
DE'KARI

Chris Green

TRIGGADALE I II III
Elijah R. Freeman
GOD BLESS THE TRAPPERS I, II, III
THESE SCANDALOUS STREETS I, II, III
FEAR MY GANGSTA I, II, III IV
THESE STREETS DON'T LOVE NOBODY I, II
BURY ME A G I, II, III, IV, V
A GANGSTA'S EMPIRE I, II, III, IV
THE DOPEMAN'S BODYGAURD I II
Tranay Adams
THE STREETS ARE CALLING
Duquie Wilson
MARRIED TO A BOSS... I II III
By Destiny Skai & Chris Green
KINGZ OF THE GAME I II III IV
Playa Ray
SLAUGHTER GANG I II III
RUTHLESS HEART I II III
By Willie Slaughter
FUK SHYT
By Blakk Diamond
DON'T F#CK WITH MY HEART I II
By Linnea
ADDICTED TO THE DRAMA I II III
By Jamila
YAYO I II III
A SHOOTER'S AMBITION I II

188

City of Kingz

By S. Allen
TRAP GOD

By Troublesome
FOREVER GANGSTA
GLOCKS ON SATIN SHEETS I II

By Adrian Dulan
TOE TAGZ I II III

By Ah'Million
KINGPIN DREAMS I II

By Paper Boi Rari
CONFESSIONS OF A GANGSTA

By Nicholas Lock
I'M NOTHING WITHOUT HIS LOVE

By Monet Dragun
CAUGHT UP IN THE LIFE I II

By Robert Baptiste
NEW TO THE GAME I II III

By **Malik D. Rice**
LIFE OF A SAVAGE I II III
A GANGSTA'S QUR'AN

By **Romell Tukes**
LOYALTY AIN'T PROMISED

By Keith Williams
QUIET MONEY I II
THUG LIFE

By **Trai'Quan**
THE STREETS MADE ME I II

Chris Green

By **Larry D. Wright**
THE ULTIMATE SACRIFICE I, II, III, IV, V
KHADIFI
IF YOU CROSS ME ONCE
By **Anthony Fields**
THE LIFE OF A HOOD STAR
By **Ca$h & Rashia Wilson**

BOOKS BY LDP'S CEO, CA$H

TRUST IN NO MAN

TRUST IN NO MAN 2

TRUST IN NO MAN 3

BONDED BY BLOOD

SHORTY GOT A THUG

THUGS CRY

THUGS CRY 2

THUGS CRY 3

TRUST NO BITCH

TRUST NO BITCH 2

TRUST NO BITCH 3

TIL MY CASKET DROPS

RESTRAINING ORDER

RESTRAINING ORDER 2

IN LOVE WITH A CONVICT

LIFE OF A HOOD STAR

Coming Soon

BONDED BY BLOOD 2

BOW DOWN TO MY GANGSTA

Chris Green